THE PROVING GROUND

Also by Elaine Marie Alphin

The Ghost Cadet

THE PROVING GROUND

ELAINE MARIE ALPHIN

HENRY HOLT AND COMPANY • NEW YORK

First edition
Published by Henry Holt and Company, Inc.,
115 West 18th Street, New York, New York 10011.
Published simultaneously in Canada by Fitzhenry & Whiteside Ltd.,
91 Granton Drive, Richmond Hill, Ontario L4B 2N5.

Library of Congress Cataloging-in-Publication Data
Alphin, Elaine Marie.
The proving ground / Elaine Marie Alphin.
Summary: While trying to adjust to life at a new military base in
a town where the residents hate the Army, Kevin, the son of a
Lieutenant Colonel, uncovers a plot to destroy the base.
ISBN 0-8050-2140-X
[1. United States. Army—Fiction. 2. Prejudices—Fiction.] I. Title.
PZ7.A4625Pr 1992   [Fic]—dc20   92-11356

Printed in the United States of America
on acid-free paper. ∞
1   3   5   7   9   10   8   6   4   2

For Art,
who knows when to stand up
and what for and what it costs

And for my own
Horatio, Hamlet, and Hannibal

CONTENTS

THE PROVING GROUND

≡ 1 ≡
MEMBERS ONLY

Kevin couldn't take his eyes off her hair. When her fist shot out, she snapped her head sideways and the long hair whipped past like a comet's tail. Fierce green eyes flashed out before the hair swept down again in front of them. She looked beautiful.

A boy worked his way to the front of the crowd watching the fight. He elbowed past Kevin as though he didn't exist. Kevin glared at the back of the stranger's denim jacket but kept his mouth shut. Kids had been doing that all day.

"Hey, quit, Charley," the boy called out. Kevin thought he sounded amused. Maybe he felt sorry for the guy being creamed by the girl.

The girl shook her head and the red hair flew as the boy in front of her smashed into a row of lockers.

"No way," she grunted. Then the guy she had pinned against the lockers took advantage of her attention shift to throw his weight against her and shove her back. She kicked one of his legs out from under him and the two of them thudded down, rolling across the floor as a couple of kids cheered.

Kevin caught his breath and edged forward, ready to jerk the kid off her. He wanted to sling him against the lockers and make him leave her alone. Not that the girl needed any help—she knew how to stand up for herself. But in his mind Kevin could see Orion draw his sword and leap into the battle. Orion was Kevin's Dungeons & Dragons character, a sixth-level Ranger. Kevin knew Orion would never let a girl fight alone, not even a warrior maiden who outranked him. He'd finish off the troll, then offer the maiden his sword in eternal fealty.

Gasping, the troll got the upper hand for a second and Kevin saw his face for the first time. It was Chris Waverly, the only ninth grader besides Kevin whose father was in the Army. With a sinking feeling, Kevin could hear his father's voice playing like a tinny tape in the back of his head: "Military families stick together, Kevin. Remember, I have to work with these people. That means you have to get along with their kids. We have to support each other." Kevin understood what his father meant. Soldiers in combat *had* to stick together. They depended on each other for their very lives. And even though it was peacetime, career officers stuck together.

The Army was just different from the civilian world; Kevin had grown up accepting that peculiarity. When other kids goofed up, they got yelled at and maybe grounded—no big deal. When an Army kid goofed up, the word went all around the military post, and he wasn't the only one in deep trouble. His father would get read the riot act by his commanding officer, and then he came home and read it to his kid.

It wasn't so much that Kevin was scared of his father's coming down hard on him. He simply respected his father too much to let himself goof up and embarrass him very often. Sometimes, though, having to watch his every move drove Kevin crazy. He felt like he'd somehow been drafted into the Army before he'd been born. There seemed to be some sort of unwritten rule that military families were under just as strict command as the military officer himself. Kevin didn't have a choice about getting along with other military kids—he had to.

Kevin knew his father would expect him to stick by Chris. What Kevin thought about the girl wasn't important enough to go out on a limb for. Getting involved in a fight on the first day of school was not what his father, or the Army, would consider getting along.

Kevin squeezed past a couple of jeering kids and leaned against the wall. He wanted to forget his father and the Army, and just stand there and watch her a little while longer. What had the other guy called her? Charley? She was too beautiful for a name like that.

Then Chris crashed to the floor and the girl was on her knees, straddling him. Her blouse had pulled out of her belt in the back, and at the sight of it Kevin felt an unfamiliar heat rush through him.

Chris cursed and twisted under her, struggling to break her grasp and knock her down, but she got a knee on one of his arms and grabbed his other wrist and twisted it backward. She punched him in the chest, hard.

"Had enough?" Her voice was sharp and angry, but something else, an underlying warm intensity in her tone, made the words echo inside Kevin's head.

"Okay!" Chris gasped.

She let go and stood up gracefully, stepping over him as though he were a cockroach she had just squashed. She wiped her hands on her tight jeans and firmly tucked her blouse back into place. Kevin grinned to himself. She hadn't needed him after all—he didn't have to feel guilty about following his father's orders and leaving her to win her own fight. Chris just lay there at her feet, coughing shakily.

"Just remember," she told him, "you keep out of my way."

She smoothed out the dark red hair and flipped it neatly over her shoulder. Then she took her books back from a girlfriend and threw Chris one last fierce glance.

"Stupid Army brat," she said.

She turned sharply and headed down the hall, not bothering to look back. Some of the kids followed her; a few even laughed at Chris, still on the floor. The rest of them went off to their buses as though the fight had never happened.

Kevin's chest felt heavy, like he had stopped breathing without noticing. Why did she call Chris an Army brat? For that matter, why were they fighting in the first place? For a second Kevin considered turning his back

on the whole thing and going to look for the Dungeons &
Dragons meeting, but he knew he couldn't just leave
Chris there. His father's voice echoed in the back of his
head: "Military families have to stick together, Kevin."
Yes, Sir, Kevin thought with resignation. He dropped
his books on the floor and walked over to Chris.

"You all right?" he asked.

The boy's head snapped up warily. Then he recognized Kevin. "Oh, you're the new kid, right? The Lieutenant Colonel's son? Yeah, I'm okay."

Kevin groaned inside. Why make a big deal out of his
father's rank? He was just another Army kid. But Chris's
father was a Captain, and Kevin's was his new boss. That
must have been why Chris hadn't bothered to introduce
himself on the school bus that morning. They were the
only two kids who got on in the Proving Ground, but
Chris had walked right past him and taken a seat alone in
the back.

"My name's Kevin Spencer."

Chris studied him for a minute. "Chris Waverly. Give
me a hand up?"

"Sure." Kevin hauled the other boy to his feet. "What
were you two fighting about, anyway?"

Chris rubbed his wrist where the girl had twisted it.
"She doesn't like Army kids."

Kevin stared at him. "Come on, that's no reason for a
fight like that. Anyway, she's a girl." He struggled to
keep his voice even. The last thing he wanted was for
Chris to realize just how impressed he was with the girl.

Chris snorted. "Yeah, well, you'll forget that when Charley has you pinned to the floor, I guarantee."

"I'm not planning on fighting her," Kevin said softly. He had a brief memory of her hair flying across her face.

Chris shrugged and bent stiffly to pick up his books. "Maybe not now, but once she finds out you're Army, she'll get you too."

"Why?"

"Her family owned farmland where the Proving Ground is now," Chris said, as though that explained it. "Anyway, most people in town can't stand the Army. First we took their land to build the Proving Ground, and now we make noise all day testing ammunition. They like the Civil Service jobs there, but they'd just as soon the whole thing was civilian-run and the green-suiters all disappeared. Come on, I'll show you where our bus picks up."

"No, I'm staying," Kevin said. "There's a D&D Club meeting I thought I'd go to. Maybe I'll join."

Chris stared at him. "Are you crazy or something? Army kids don't join things in Hadley."

"Why not?" Kevin asked, wondering which one of them was crazy. They didn't both seem to be in the same conversation.

"Town groups and school clubs are for Hadley kids," Chris said. His voice was slow and patient, as though he were explaining something obvious to a little kid.

"Well, for the rest of Dad's assignment here I'm a Hadley kid," Kevin told him.

Chris shook his head. "Never. Once an Army kid,

always an Army kid. You'll never fit into Hadley. You've got to be born here to belong to anything."

Kevin wondered if he should believe Chris and go on home with him. Would going with the other military kid instead of joining the town club fall under his father's rule that military families had to stick together? But Kevin really liked Dungeons & Dragons. Orion had been a star character with the kids who'd played at Fort Carson. Kevin wanted to give him a chance in a new universe. His father would just have to understand.

"Thanks," he said finally, "but I'll give it a try."

Chris shrugged. "Good luck," he said. "You'll need it."

Kevin watched him jog stiffly down the empty hall toward the parking lot. Why should he need luck joining a school club? he wondered. And why was Charley so angry at Army kids? The Army hadn't stolen those farms, after all. The Government *had* paid for them.

Kevin shook his head and went over to pick up his books. Hadley, Indiana, seemed like the strangest town he'd ever moved to, and he had been a new kid in a lot of places. With his father getting a different assignment every two or three years, Kevin had changed schools and towns so often he thought he was used to it.

But his first day at this school had been weird. He felt invisible. None of the other ninth graders spoke to him; none of the teachers made any fuss over introducing the new class member after the Christmas vacation. They all seemed to be ignoring him.

And yet, there was something about Hadley he

couldn't help liking. He got the feeling that the people who ignored him were complete together. They didn't need outsiders. They'd known each other all their lives, entire families knowing each other stretching back generations. They all belonged in Hadley, and Hadley belonged to them.

Kevin wondered how that would feel, living somewhere all your life like that and having family around—knowing you were walking where your parents and grandparents and great-grandparents had walked. He sometimes wished his father had never joined the Army, never left the town he had grown up in. Kevin thought he'd like to live within walking distance of his grandparents, and know kids whose parents had played with his parents when they were kids.

But no one in Hadley cared that he wished he were like them. Kevin had the strangest feeling that no one in Hadley wanted him there at all.

Well, he thought as he hurried downstairs, no one had asked Kevin Spencer if he wanted to come to Indiana, either. It looked like both Hadley and Kevin were going to have to make the best of it. He found the classroom where the Dungeons & Dragons Club met with no trouble, and eased through the open door. None of the kids noticed him.

Kevin studied the different Dungeons & Dragons figures spread out on the large game-board grid. He took quick glances at the other kids, checking for anybody he recognized from that first day. He drew blanks until he saw Charley.

She was pulling intricately carved wooden D&D models from a box, talking excitedly to a couple of other girls. Her whole body talked with her, and that fiery red hair swirled behind her. Kevin wished she'd look up at him with those piercing green eyes. He wanted her to talk to him the way she was talking about D&D strategy right now.

"Hi," a tall boy said.

Kevin looked up with a start. He'd stopped expecting anybody to notice him.

"You need something?" the boy asked.

"Hi," Kevin said. He cleared his throat. "Ah, I'm new here. I wanted to join your D&D club. I've got a sixth-level ranger named Orion. Oh, my name's Kevin Spencer."

The boy grinned and pushed his glasses higher on the bridge of his nose. "We can always use new players, especially with sixth-level characters. I'm this month's Dungeon Master, Andy Farris. Where'd you move from?"

"Colorado, near Colorado Springs," Kevin said, relieved. Maybe Chris was wrong. Maybe the cold shoulders all day had been in his imagination. Maybe the kids were just waiting for him to make the first move.

"How do you like Hadley?" Andy asked.

Kevin couldn't begin to put into words the confusion he felt about the town. "Uh, it's really nice," he managed.

"Where do you live?"

"On the Proving Ground," Kevin said.

There was a dead silence.

Charley put down the carved dragon she was holding and turned to look directly at him, just as Kevin had hoped. But she wasn't smiling.

"You're the new Army kid," she said in a low voice. "The one who moved into Quarters 12."

"Yeah," Kevin said, trying to smile. "We got here over Christmas vacation."

"And you want to join our Dungeons & Dragons Club?" she demanded.

"Sure," Kevin said. "I used to play in my old school."

"Well," Andy began.

"You're not suggesting he join?" Charley interrupted, her voice rising.

"Ease up, Charley," Andy said quietly. "He can play with us if he wants."

Kevin looked back and forth at the two of them. What was going on? Everything had been fine, they were treating him just like any other new kid, and then bang—he said he lived on the Proving Ground and it was like he'd confessed to having the plague or something.

"If he joins, I'm quitting," Charley announced.

The other kids looked at one another uncertainly. Two girls fussed with their books for a moment, then wandered over to stand behind Charley. They looked back at Kevin with their chins raised and their books clutched across their chests. Kevin could feel how much they liked Charley, and he knew they didn't care enough about him to stand up to her. He didn't even know how to begin to argue his case. He could see that Charley was confident none of the kids would ever let her quit, not over him. She swept her hair back and put her hands on her hips, and stared coldly at him.

"You want some advice, Army brat?" she demanded.

"My name's Kevin," he told her, and heard his voice crack.

"I don't care what your name is," Charley said, her eyes flashing. "You just remember this: Nobody in Hadley wants you here."

Kevin backed away from her, stunned. She seemed to be voicing his worst fears, making them real. But one kid couldn't speak for the whole town. Or could she? His textbooks felt slippery in his hand, and he could feel his shirt sticking damply to his back.

She *hates* me, he realized. Why?

"So stay inside the Proving Ground," Charley went on, "and stick to your own kind. Keep away from the rest of us!"

She turned her back on him and reached into her box again. She took out an elegant wizard and a noble fighter, and set them down beside the dragon. She was concentrating so completely on her figures that Kevin felt as though she'd swept him out of existence.

Kevin made himself turn and shut the door behind him. He stood blindly in the hallway trying to sort out feelings that chased each other sickeningly in angry circles. It hurt to breathe, as though someone had snapped his ribs and was sticking the sharp points into his lungs. Sickened at how easily he'd let himself be hurt, Kevin clenched his fists and used his anger to force in huge gulps of air despite the pain in his chest. His anger at his father for moving him to Hadley—one breath. His anger at himself, for his voice breaking when he'd tried to stand up to Charley—another breath. His anger at Charley herself, for hating him when he liked her so much—a deep breath.

Who does she think she is? he thought, new fury sweeping away the sharp ache inside. How dare she? She's not going to get away with this—

"Hey, you all right?"

Kevin jumped and twisted around to see Andy.

"Look," the other boy said, "I'm sorry about Charley. She's got a grudge against the Army people at the Proving Ground."

Kevin shrugged and looked away. Even if Orion were beaten in combat, he wouldn't whine. He'd find some reason to swagger. Kevin held on to his anger and made his voice hard. "Who cares? What kind of a name for a girl is Charley, anyway?"

Andy grinned. "Her name's Charlene Hanson, actually, but everybody calls her Charley. Can you imagine her as Charlene?"

"No," Kevin said tightly, hearing her taunting voice calling him Army brat. "More like a Chuck, I'd say."

Andy laughed, then got serious. "Look, not everybody feels like Charley does. Give it some time, you'll settle in."

"What's she got against the Proving Ground, any-way?" Kevin asked.

Andy studied him. "Her family used to live out there. But when the Government took the land to build the Proving Ground, they made her family move."

"Well, I didn't have anything to do with it," Kevin snapped. "Why is she out to get me?"

"She said you were living in Quarters 12," Andy said. He took his glasses off and started to polish one lens on the tail of his shirt. "Is that right?"

Kevin nodded. "So what?"

Andy put his glasses back on.

"So you're living in her house."

≡ 2 ≡

LOCAL HISTORY

It was the end of the week before Kevin got the chance to find out what Andy meant. His father had a tank gun test scheduled for Friday evening, and Mrs. Spencer was planning a late dinner. Kevin told his mother he'd take his bike to school instead of the bus and be home late. He'd decided to do a little research at the library after school.

For the end of January it was good biking weather. Most places would have had too much snow for a long bike ride, but the southern Indiana weather was clear and cold. Kevin hadn't seen any snow since they came to Hadley.

He took his heels off his bike pedals and watched them whirl as he coasted downhill. One week of school over, nineteen to go. Kevin was pretty sure they couldn't get much worse. The Hadley kids seemed out to get him. And it was nothing he could fight—he still seemed invisible. Someone always happened to wander by and slam his locker shut when he tried to switch books, someone seemed to slide into every classroom seat he started to take, and he regularly found himself elbowed to the back of the lunch line. But nobody ever looked him in the eye when they did it, just pushed past him or slid into his seat as though he didn't exist.

The first time somebody took his seat, Kevin had said something, but the kid had stared through him, and then the teacher had bustled in and told Kevin to get seated so he could start the class. Kevin had caught the sleeve of one guy who slammed his locker and started to ask, "Hey, what gives?" but the kid jerked his arm away, shrugged, and called back, "Must've got in my way." Trying to argue, trying to make anyone admit they were doing anything, was like fighting the wind.

But Kevin had realized a few things that first week. As the long Indiana hill flattened out, he slipped his feet back onto his pedals and started pumping so as not to lose speed. One of the things he had learned was that there were two distinct crowds, and only one of them was freezing him out. The other crowd just didn't seem to realize he existed. That one was made up of kids like Andy Farris, whose fathers worked for Dow Corning or Somerset Manufacturing or Arvin Industries. These businesses were in Asherton, and Hadley was a kind of bedroom community for the people who worked there. Every few years those people were transferred to a new office, so their kids were used to being new themselves. Kevin figured they weren't too different from Army kids in that respect. They brushed past him in the halls without saying anything, but he was beginning to think it wasn't because they hated him. Maybe they just hadn't had any reason to notice him yet.

Kevin signaled and swung his bike onto Main Street. If there had been a lot of Army kids here, one of them would have taken him up to the others and said, "This is Kevin—his dad works with mine," and then the other kids would have made room for him at their lunch table. Probably that's how the Dow Corning kids and the Somerset kids and the Arvin kids got to know new-comers too. Kevin didn't exist for them, because none of them knew who he was.

Except Andy. Twice Kevin saw him in the hall. Once Andy had grinned and waved. The second time he stopped, and Kevin thought he was going to come over and say something, but the warning bell rang. Andy had groaned and sprinted for class. Kevin thought maybe if he could connect with Andy the other transplant kids would notice him, and school would end up okay.

Classes weren't too bad. Even sitting in the back corner in every room Kevin had already scored a 9.4 on a history pop quiz and gotten a $B+$ on an English theme. The best moment had been acing a geometry quiz and having the teacher look at him instead of through him. Kevin had been on the Math Team at his old school at Fort Carson. Joining the Math Team in Hadley was probably as empty a dream as joining the Dungeons & Dragons Club, but the quiz was a bright reminder that he was still the same guy. Only the kids around him were different.

Kevin jumped the curb and coasted up to the library. He chained his bike to the railing and pushed through a pair of heavy swinging doors. The library was small and dark, and he could see shadowy stacks in the back. After he finished his research he might look around. He could probably find some old science fiction to take home. But first he needed some reference help.

"Hi," he said, smiling politely at the librarian. She was sitting on a high stool inside a circular desk in the middle of the front room, with a thick book of fairy tales propped up in front of her.

"I'm doing research for a history project in school, and I was hoping you could help me. I need some information about the Proving Ground. Are there some old newspapers or other stuff I could look through?"

She eyed him curiously over the top of the book for a few seconds, then nodded toward the back. "Climb up that iron staircase. We have the family genealogies and the local-newspaper-clipping files up there. Just look under Hadley Proving Ground. It's all in alphabetical order."

"Thanks." Kevin quickly started toward the back.

"Just a minute," she called after him.

Kevin turned around, dreading her question. He'd hoped he wouldn't have to admit he was the new Army kid until after he'd finished his research. The librarian probably wouldn't be very helpful once she knew.

"If there's anything you want copies of," she said, "just bring the file down here and show me. I'll photocopy them for you for five cents each."

"Thanks," Kevin said again. The relief was so strong he felt painfully hot inside his quilted jacket. "I may need some copies."

He found the curving wrought-iron staircase in the far corner, behind the fiction stacks, and climbed up. The upper level must have been added on, he decided. It was a metal grillwork floor bolted into the walls. All there seemed to be was a lot of file cabinets and two tables to work on. Kevin dropped his jacket and backpack onto one of the tables and checked the file cabinets. He avoided the family genealogies and found the local history files. He was in luck—there were three thick file folders labeled HADLEY PROVING GROUND. Kevin pulled them all out and carried them over to the table.

Inside the folders the clippings didn't seem to be in any sort of order. He flipped through them for a while, trying to figure out what happened when. As nearly as he could work out, the Government had been looking for a site for a new ordnance testing ground for a couple of years before they chose Hadley at the end of 1940. Even though the United States wasn't actually involved in World War II yet, Kevin reasoned, the War Department probably knew they'd be in it before too long, and they needed to have the new testing facility ready before then.

Everybody had been pretty optimistic in the beginning, it seemed. The government had mapped out over 40,000 acres for the Proving Ground, and everybody owning land there had been told to move the following spring. But then things started going wrong. The officials checking the land deeds in order to establish the prices on people's property were caught trying to juggle figures so they could take a big cut off the top from the settlement payments. All payments to landowners stopped while a new commission was set up to straighten out the mess and start over—but progress on the Proving Ground didn't stop. That meant a lot of people were turned out of their homes with no check from the government.

Kevin sat back and thought about the rusty cars and the kids in faded overalls he kept seeing around town. The Proving Ground takeover had been fifty years ago, but he was willing to bet that most of the families had been no better off than the farm families were now. If anything, they probably had less money. And he was sure that most of them didn't have enough savings in a bank to just turn around and buy a new place without that government check. He shook his head over the brittle newspapers. No wonder people had felt hostile about the high-handed way the Army had thrown them out.

Once a family was moved out of their home, he discovered, they weren't allowed to return to the Proving Ground for anything without getting special permission from the Adjutant's office, and generally being made to feel pretty small. Kevin knew how depressing it felt to try to go up against the military bureaucracy even if you were part of the system. So if these people found they'd forgotten something from their old house, it wasn't a simple matter of calling up the new owners and telling them to send it or to let them come back and look for it, like it would be for most people. They had to beg the Army to let them go back to their family home. Kevin cringed at the thought.

It was even worse because these were farms. The people living there had been on the same land for generations, and moving was a real shock to them. It was lousy to move around every few years and to never feel like you belonged anywhere, Kevin thought, but it would be horrible to be taken from the only home you'd ever known, like jerking a plant out of the ground and tearing out its roots, and then jamming it into some old flowerpot and expecting it to go on as though nothing had happened. Kevin had seen his mother replant a lot of things over the years, and he knew that they didn't always survive. Some of the plants just couldn't stand the shock.

Some of the people waited until the Government wrote new checks for the property, and as soon as they had their money they just got out of Hadley for good. Some of them tried to find town jobs to take the place of their farming. In a way, the bombing of Pearl Harbor the following December probably helped people cope. There were plenty of jobs in the military, and by the time the war ended in 1945 nothing was the way it had been before, so turning their backs on their farms and their family history hadn't hurt so much. Maybe.

But not everyone took their checks and walked away.

Some landowners refused to accept the government's right to take their land. Kevin read that some of them refused to leave their property and had to be removed. If they refused to sell to the Government, they were brought to court so that their property could be condemned. It sounded as though raising objections was an exercise in futility, but if you believed something was wrong, Kevin guessed you had to take a stand. He felt a flicker of admiration for the families who wanted their objections to be known. Then he saw a familiar name.

Duane Hanson had refused to sell to the Government. He had given an interview to the newspaper, and Kevin read, "I believe that we need the Army to defend our country, and I understand that the Army needs a place to test its guns and ammunition. Maybe Hadley is the right place, maybe not. That isn't my decision. But I resent the way the U.S. Government just came in and took a chunk of land, my land, not paying any attention to the people who already lived there. They're supposed to be my government too, and I don't pay my taxes to have some government bureaucrat throw me off my homestead. That's wrong, and I want to go to court and say so."

Kevin sighed. Old Mr. Hanson sounded a lot like Charley. What was she, his granddaughter? He found a newspaper picture of the family on their old front porch. Mr. Hanson looked pretty old. He already had two adult sons, one who had been farming the family land and one who had moved out east sometime earlier. The son in the picture, Ron, had two youngsters with him, a son Earl and another son, Duane. Earl looked about five or six, and Duane was maybe ten. Kevin calculated ages. If Charley was the youngest in her family, one of the two boys was probably her father. So old Duane Hanson had been her great-grandfather.

Kevin set aside the clipping of the interview and saw an article underneath about the condemnation suit against the Hansons. There was another grainy picture, this time of Mr. Hanson testifying in court. Kevin stared at the article, shocked. Mr. Hanson had gotten his turn to speak out, but in the witness box the Government's attorney had given him a hard time. The old man had gotten angrier and angrier, trying to make himself understood, until he'd exploded. He'd had a heart attack, right there in the courtroom. The headline read CONDEMNATION SUIT DEFENDANT DIES IN WITNESS BOX.

≡ 3 ≡

WHOSE FAULT?

Kevin had the librarian copy the articles about Mr. Hanson for him. He stuffed them into his backpack and hurried out of the building without stopping to look at the stacks. The thought of asking for a library card sent a cold sweat down his back. He couldn't admit who he was. The librarian's family had probably lived in Hadley for generations. She'd hate him too.

No wonder no one liked the Army people from the Proving Ground! They'd stolen people's homes, and they'd killed an old man. Kevin fumbled the combination twice trying to unlock his bike. Every time he heard a footstep, he froze. He was petrified someone would see him and recognize him. Some hero you are, he thought, disgusted with himself. What would Orion do? Probably be smart enough to call it quits and find a different universe to play in.

Kevin clenched his hand on the lock in a surge of resentment. Why couldn't he have the same option? Why did he have to get dragged along wherever the Army decided to send his father?

Then he thought of Charley's hatred of him. How

could he blame her for feeling the way she did? Kevin's Army had killed her great-grandfather. Well, it really wasn't the Army, it was the bureaucracy, but obviously that distinction hadn't mattered to the rest of the Hansons the way it had to the old man. And as if his death weren't enough, the Hanson family house had been turned into officers' quarters. The Hansons had to live with the knowledge that the people who were responsible for Duane Hanson's death were living comfortably in the house that should be their home. That was what Andy had been trying to tell him.

Kevin finally freed his bike and hit the street with a running start. He didn't even care about the long haul uphill to the Proving Ground. All he wanted to do was get home. He'd like to get out of Hadley if he could, but right now he'd settle for just getting back inside the Proving Ground fence.

His brakes screeched as the light turned red on Main Street. Kevin squeezed his handlebars and told himself the high school kids didn't hang out downtown. Nobody was going to recognize him. But the instant the light turned green he shot across the intersection.

What do I do now? he asked himself. Who do I tell? And what are they going to do about it?

Times like this are when you really need a friend, he thought. At Fort Carson he'd bummed around with Mike Golding most of the time. He turned off Main Street and imagined writing Mike a letter.

Dear Mike, he thought, how's the new post? Hadley

Proving Ground isn't exactly what I expected. You should see it—only thirteen sets of quarters, and only one other kid here my age. Not much like Fort Carson, huh? I met this terrific girl at school, but she hates Army kids. Come to think of it, everybody from Hadley hates Army people. You see, the government stole their land and killed one of their farmers fifty years ago, and the kids blame me for it. Wish you were here. . . .

He really did wish Mike was with him, but Kevin knew it was no use writing. Army friendships didn't last. Once you moved to a new post, you forgot the kids from your old post because you'd probably never see them again. Kevin's father talked about old buddies from past assignments, and sometimes they sent Christmas cards, but even those friendships weren't real, not like a friend you could tell your troubles to or call up at the last minute because you needed to talk to him, not like someone you'd grown up with and you could count on to always understand because he knew you, through and through.

The hill started to climb, and Kevin shifted gears to make the pedaling easier. It was dumb thinking about Mike, anyway. Mike had already made plenty of new friends at his father's new post, Kevin was sure of it. Here there was nobody but Chris Waverly.

Kevin breathed harder as the hill steepened. He downshifted until he ran out of gears, then stood up on the pedals to get a little extra leverage. The backpack pounded his back, as though the copies of the article on

Charley's great-grandfather weighed a ton. Kevin finally rolled to a halt and had to get off and push his bike uphill until the slope leveled out. Then he jumped on and pedaled full speed for home. Hadley might have year-round bicycling weather, but places seemed a long way apart. And of course the Proving Ground was the farthest from everything.

Kevin pumped hard on the pedals and watched the withered rows of corn flash past out of the corner of his eye. When they'd first arrived in Hadley, he'd been surprised to see the rows of cornstalks still standing. They should have been harvested long before year's end. But his father said that last summer had been unusually dry and the corn was a loss. The farmers would let it stand, and just plow it under next spring.

At the Proving Ground gate Kevin stopped his bike and pulled his military ID out of his jeans pocket. The security guard looked up from his book, glanced briefly at the ID and at Kevin, then waved him through. Kevin pocketed his ID and headed toward the Housing Area. It was nearly an extra mile to circle around through the gate and backtrack to the Housing Area, but the Proving Ground was surrounded by a security fence and barbed wire that was definitely not intended for kids to vault over and come in the back way.

Kevin finally reached his house—the Hansons' house, he thought—and put his bike into the garage. He felt cold and stiff as he went inside the house and climbed upstairs to his room. He could hear his mother in the kitchen, listening to classical music while she got dinner ready. Kevin didn't feel up to talking to her right then. He knew she'd been feeling isolated since they'd come to Hadley also, and the two of them trying to be cheerful about the situation was more than he could handle.

Upstairs Kevin dropped his backpack on his desk chair and pushed his door shut behind him, wishing he could shut out Hadley as easily. He looked over at the cage, but Hannibal was out of sight, probably sound asleep in his house.

"Come on, Hannibal," he said finally. "Say hello."

He opened the cage and took out the dish to put in some fresh food. The hamster poked his head sleepily out of his house at the noise, then stretched and came over to see what was happening. Kevin smiled a little at the sight of him, remembering the first hamster he'd ever brought home. Horatio had been the fourth-grade mascot when Kevin's father had been stationed at Fort Bliss. When summer came, none of the kids could take Horatio, so Kevin had volunteered to bring him home. His father had shaken his head at Horatio in the beginning, but the corners of his mouth tended to curl slightly at the sight of the little animal riding on Kevin's shoulder or peeking out of his pocket. In time, a hamster became an accepted member of the Spencer family.

Kids at Fort Carson had thought it was weird that Kevin had a hamster, but Kevin never let it bother him. He'd seen what happened to Army pets. When you move every couple of years and you don't have family around or a real home to tie you down, it's easy to look at a pet as a temporary arrangement, the way military quarters were only a temporary home. You get new orders moving you to a new post, you get a new pet when you get there.

Mike had had a tough little bulldog named Rommel, Kevin remembered. When they would play with the dog, Mike used to jeer, "Can't do that with a hamster!" And Kevin had agreed. But Mike's father had gotten new orders, and there would have been the hassle of moving the dog plus tons of red tape registering it at the new post, so Mike's father told him to find a new home for his pet. Mike had asked all his friends, but in the end he'd had to leave Rommel at the pound and move on.

Kevin couldn't do that—get a pet for a year or two, play with him and tame him and have him trust you, and then dump him at the pound because you couldn't move him. A hamster he could move when his father got new orders.

When Kevin put the food dish back in place, he reached over and picked up the little animal. So what if it's a little weird, he thought. I like hamsters!

"Hi, Hannibal," he said softly, stroking the golden fur. "You know what? This place is worse than I thought. Charley's great-grandfather *died* because of it. And everybody acts like it's all my fault."

Hannibal sighed and yawned, and nuzzled against Kevin's shirt.

"You want to take another nap?" Kevin sat down against the wall and lifted the hamster up to his shoulder. Hannibal sniffed around for a minute, then he climbed up Kevin's shoulder and ran along his collar to the back of his neck. He rustled around for a while, then curled himself up and drifted back to sleep. Kevin could feel the soft fur brushing his neck as the little animal breathed.

"I don't know what to do, Hannibal," Kevin said. He thought the Government had been wrong, and he couldn't blame the people who got screwed for being mad at the Army and hating the people who did it to them. But why hold on to it? It certainly wasn't his fault, or even his father's, that Charley's great-grandfather died during the trial. It wasn't even the Army's fault, come to think of it—hadn't that been what Duane Hanson had been trying to explain to the reporter? It was the Federal Government, the bureaucracy, that ran over the little people like the Hansons.

Kevin stared across the room, thinking about Charley, remembering the swirl of long red hair and her intense green eyes. He'd never seen any girl like her before. Yeah, he told himself, and you're not going to be seeing much of her in the future if you're smart. You may like her, but she hates you like poison, so keep away.

He sighed and shifted against the wall, unsettling Hannibal. The hamster shook himself and climbed down Kevin's shirt, looking for someplace more peaceful to sleep.

"Sorry, fellow," Kevin said. He grabbed a couple of cubes of dried food and dropped them in his shirt pocket. "Take a nap in here, okay?"

Hannibal stretched and sniffed, then climbed down into the familiar pocket. He turned around a couple of times, then went back to sleep. Kevin buttoned the flap over him and wandered over to look out his window into the darkening twilight.

The Proving Ground was huge, plenty of land for the Army to test its ammunition and weapons without any danger of hurting anybody. It was like living in some kind of state park, Kevin thought. He could see deer feeding back behind the houses. There were probably plenty of other animals, too. It could be a really neat place to live, with all that countryside to explore and animals to watch. At least, it would be if there were somebody to explore with. Kevin turned away from the window. Even if things got better at school, he couldn't imagine finding anybody in Hadley who'd want to come explore the Proving Ground with him.

"Stop feeling sorry for yourself," he muttered angrily, knowing he was stuck here for two years whether he liked it or not. His father had his head buried in his work, and his mother was bound to find some wives' social world for herself sooner or later, but he was on his own.

"Kevin!" his mother called from downstairs. "Your father's home—come on down for dinner."

Kevin turned away from the window. Showtime, he

thought. Now we all sit around the table and pretend we love Hadley and everything's going great.

⟨ He clattered down the stairs, trying not to bounce Hannibal too badly. Actually, the hamster was so used to sleeping in his shirt pocket they could probably ride a roller coaster like this and Hannibal wouldn't wake up.

"So, how do you like Hadley?" Kevin's father asked at the dinner table.

Kevin's mother put down her fork and sighed. "If I hear that question from one more person in this town, I think I'll scream." She shook her head. "Wherever I go, they ask that, and as soon as they find out we live on the Proving Ground, their eyes just sort of go out of focus and somehow they start talking to somebody else. I don't know if it's my imagination or what, but I feel invisible around here."

Kevin recognized the feeling.

"The Proving Ground isn't very popular with the townspeople, that's for sure," LTC Spencer said wearily. "What about you, Kevin? How's school?"

Kevin shrugged and concentrated on his plate. "School's okay," he said. "Pretty much like any other school, I guess."

"Have you made any friends yet?" his mother asked.

Kevin scrunched his nose at her. "Come on, Mom, I'm not a little kid. You don't need to worry about me settling in. It takes a while to get involved, that's all, especially moving here in the middle of the school year like this." He avoided mentioning that he didn't think he'd be getting involved anytime in the next two years, until they moved again.

"There's another boy about your age living in one of the other sets of quarters," his father said.

"Yeah, Chris Waverly," Kevin told them. "I met him at school already. He's okay, I guess." He didn't think they'd want to know Chris had gotten beaten up by a girl.

"I would have thought he'd have come by and introduced himself before school started," his mother said.

"His father works for me," LTC Spencer said shortly. Then he sighed. "Anyway, people seem to keep to themselves around here. Have many of the wives come over to meet you?"

She shook her head. "One so far. Not like Fort Carson."

"What about you, Dad?" Kevin asked. "What about work?"

His parents glanced at each other. "It's not quite like any assignment I've had before," his father said carefully. "I'm not commanding troops here, I'm managing civilians."

Kevin looked up. What his father loved about the Army was getting out in the field and working with troops. No wonder he wasn't very happy about coming to Hadley. Then Kevin realized what managing civilians meant. "You mean the people who live in town work for you?"

"A lot of them, yes."

Kevin whistled. "The people who you said didn't like the Proving Ground?"

"I didn't say they didn't like it," his father said. "They work here, so I have to assume they like the fact that it provides jobs. I said the Proving Ground wasn't very popular with them. I guess I should have said the Army isn't very popular."

"No kidding," Kevin said. He decided to take the plunge and tell his father about Charley's great-grandfather. Maybe he would know what Kevin could do to make peace with Charley.

"I was reading about the Proving Ground at the library today—how they fouled up buying the land and about the condemnation suits. I read about the man who died at his trial, Mr. Hanson," Kevin said. "His great-granddaughter goes to school with me. You could say the Army isn't very popular with her."

"Hanson?" His father frowned, thinking. "I have an Earl Hanson working in one of my test divisions, in demolitions. He's a little surly, but no more so than any of the others. This girl could be a relative. Is she giving you trouble, Kevin?"

There was no good answer to that one. Kevin decided to sidestep the question. "They kind of have a point, Dad. I mean, taking the land for the Proving Ground didn't go very smoothly."

"Nothing does," LTC Spencer said shortly. "Yes, Kevin, they have a point. The bureaucracy was high-handed and a lot of people got insulted. But the time to complain was then. A lot of things are unfair. You raise your objection, you try to get things straightened out, then you move ahead with your life. You can't look behind you forever and blame the past for all your troubles today."

Kevin thought about it. That made sense. In fact, that sounded a lot like what old Duane Hanson had intended to do. But he hadn't lived long enough to raise his objections. Kevin could see how having something in the past left unfinished could eat away at the Hanson family until it drove them slightly crazy. He felt Hannibal moving around inside his pocket and wondered if the hamster could smell their dinner. He hoped he'd put enough food in his pocket or he'd end up with a hamster on the dinner table and two annoyed parents.

Then he thought about their conversation again and realized he hadn't been paying attention to what his father was saying besides answering his questions.

"Earl Hanson is surly like the others? What's going on, Dad? Are these people making things hard for you at work?"

Kevin's father speared the last of his chicken. "Oh, they don't make trouble, really. Hanson is actually a pretty good worker. These people just don't like the way the military does things. They tend to slow operations down, and they don't take what we're doing here very seriously. They can't seem to understand that if our tests aren't one hundred percent reliable, bad ammunition or gun tubes can get out in the field and people can get killed. Some manufacturer's rep offers them free company caps or coffee mugs, and they figure it's peacetime so they get a little lax about testing his ammunition. It might help if the commander and the other officers here took a different attitude, but everybody seems so shortsighted—and the security is appalling—" He interrupted himself as though he had said more than he intended.

Kevin stared at him, surprised. "What do you mean? They've got more security here than I've ever seen before in my life. Every time we drive in past that cyclone fence with the barbed wire on top and have to stop and show our IDs to the guard at the gate, I feel like I'm going inside some sort of prison."

"Well, we're unusual in that we show our IDs," his father said. "Most of the other people who live here or work here just breeze through and wave at the guards and expect to be recognized. Some of the security guards already recognize my pickup truck and just wave me through without bothering to come out and check my ID."

"What's wrong with that?" Kevin asked. "Anything that makes this place a little less like a prison can't hurt."

"The problem," his father told him sharply, "is that with all the weapons and ammunition and explosives stored inside this post, our security can't afford to let the wrong people in."

"What wrong people?" Kevin asked, bewildered. "Hadley, Indiana, isn't exactly a war zone."

His father got up from the table abruptly and carried his plate into the kitchen. Kevin's mother watched him go, then looked back at her son and sighed.

"Kevin, your father doesn't mean to sound so harsh. He's just overloaded with the Proving Ground. And there are things to do with his work that we're not supposed to discuss. You know that—different things, but it's always the same, wherever we are."

Kevin nodded, concentrating on the last of his broccoli. "Yeah, I know, Mom, but Dad usually explains when he wants us to do something. Since we got here, he's started snapping orders like Napoleon."

Mrs. Spencer winced but nodded. "Point taken. But don't fight him on the security issue, please, Kevin? Just take his word for it that whatever security requirements there are on this post exist for a reason, and don't give the guards any trouble."

"I wouldn't!" Kevin said, insulted. "I've never hassled an MP in my life!"

He shoved his chair back from the table. "I'm through. Can I be excused?"

His mother nodded again.

Kevin grabbed his dishes and dumped them in the kitchen sink. Then he went into the living room and stared out the large front window at the dark Proving Ground. His father hadn't always been so short tempered and bossy. Kevin could remember when he was little—his father would come in, grubby from the field in his green fatigues, and while he cleaned up he'd tell Kevin stories about his troops, or about his two tours in Vietnam. He hadn't been too tired or too angry to talk then.

Kevin's favorite story had been about the surprise assault on the firebase in 'Nam. "I was commanding an infantry company," his father would tell him proudly. "My troops were in a defensive position on a hilltop three or four miles from the firebase." He'd take his black combat boots, still muddy from the field, and put them on top of a pile of dirty clothes to represent the infantry company. Then he'd drop his helmet on the floor beside the bed to represent the firebase.

"I heard over the radio that the unit at the firebase had been surprised by a human wave Vietcong attack," he told Kevin, surrounding his helmet by rows of attacking bath towels. "The Vietcong had charged the American soldiers at the firebase in such large numbers that they were in danger of being overrun. Although the firebase had plenty of long-range artillery, the unit didn't have enough men with rifles and machine guns to repulse the attack."

Kevin's father explained how he had listened to the frantic debate over the radio airwaves as the higher-ups wrestled with the situation. They tried to send in reinforcements by helicopter, but the weather was bad and the choppers had to turn back. No other reinforcements were close enough to march in to rescue the firebase.

"But you were," the younger Kevin would always say. "And you knew what to do!"

As soon as the confusion hit the radio waves, Kevin's

father had realized that no one else was in position to relieve the trapped soldiers. "I was sure the orders would come any minute to lead my men to the firebase," he told Kevin, "so I galvanized my company. Every soldier was organized for combat, even the mechanics and clerks, and every weapon was readied, even the antiaircraft machine gun on the cook's truck."

"But the orders didn't come, did they?" Kevin would prompt, eager to participate in the familiar story.

His father would shake his head. "I waited as long as I could, but when the choppers had to turn back, I took it upon myself. I knew I was supposed to stay on the hilltop, but I made the decision to march to the sound of the guns," he would say, taking the combat boots and marching them down off the dirty laundry to rescue the surrounded helmet.

Then he'd pause with one boot raised in midstep, and look at Kevin seriously. "I didn't have the authority to do what I did, but someone had to take action. You may not be the man who's supposed to make the decision, but sometimes you have to, just because you're there. And you have to take the responsibility for that decision." He would stare at the poised combat boot, and his expression would harden. "If the enemy had been waiting for us when we marched off the hilltop, or if I had failed in the rescue, I could have been responsible for losing the lives of the men in my company. In that case, I probably would have been court-martialed for leaving my position without orders."

"But you didn't fail!" Kevin would cheer. Knowing the ending had never made the story any less satisfying, no matter how many times he heard it. "You rescued the firebase!"

"Yes!" his father would shout back, and they'd laugh together as the boots stomped decisively on the bath towels around the helmet—but then his father would get serious again. "Remember, Kevin, I took a risk, but I didn't just sail stupidly into battle. I had every man, rifle, and machine gun I could muster. My mortars and my other support weapons were ready. I advanced carefully, ready to pull into a defensive position if I had to. Even though I was taking a risk, I wanted everything possible in my favor. I didn't just blindly rush off. You have to be prepared, or your people will die. Do you understand, Kevin?"

And Kevin would nod and say, "Yeah, Dad—don't go off half-cocked." But inside he'd be thinking, Someday I'll do that, Dad. I'll make the decision and I'll take the responsibility for it, and I'll be a hero too. . . .

Kevin sighed at the memory. These days his father wore a green suit with a tie instead of field fatigues, and he snapped orders instead of telling stories. And Kevin didn't think he'd get to be any sort of hero himself anymore. That was just for Orion.

He turned away from the dark window and picked up the local evening paper to read the comics. Before he found them, he saw an article with HADLEY PROVING GROUND in the headline, and read it curiously.

"So that's what you didn't want to tell me," he called to his parents.

"What?" LTC Spencer came into the living room, frowning.

"Look." Kevin pointed at the article. "You're getting terrorist threats, huh? That's why you're so worried about security?"

"Let me see that." Kevin's father grabbed the newspaper and skimmed the article. "I don't believe this! How the hell did the paper find out about it?"

"Is it some big terrorist group?" Kevin asked eagerly, wishing his father would talk to him like the old days. "Some antinuke people—no, that can't be it because you said there aren't any nuclear weapons here, right?"

"This is no joke, Kevin," his father said sharply. "It was just a threat, and I don't believe anything will come of it, but I don't like it spread all over the newspapers." He strode to the front hall and reached for his coat. "I'm going over to my office."

Then he stopped with his coat in his hand and turned back. "Look, Kevin, I don't mean to get on your case about security. I know you don't understand the problems here on post and I don't want you to have to worry about them. Just believe me when I say I've got some severe troubles here, and security is one of them. Now, I want your word you'll keep quiet about this terrorist business at school."

"Sure," Kevin said. "No problem."

He watched his father leave, perplexed. Why would

his father be so insistent he keep quiet about something he didn't even know anything about? Then he unbuttoned his shirt pocket and took out Hannibal. "It's not as though anybody at school is going to ask me," he told him as they went back upstairs. "Nobody there talks to me enough to ask any questions."

But Kevin had plenty of questions himself. Who would make terrorist threats against Hadley Proving Ground? If it wasn't some big international group, who else would want to threaten the post? Kevin couldn't help thinking that there seemed to be plenty of people in the town of Hadley who would probably be overjoyed if something happened to the Proving Ground. But would any of them go around making terrorist threats?

≡ 4 ≡

APOLOGIES NOT ACCEPTED

When Andy made the first move to get Kevin involved in Hadley High School, he took Kevin completely by surprise. Kevin was standing by his locker after his last class, trying to decide what to do about the kid slouching against the wall a couple of lockers down. The guy was chewing gum and staring up at the ceiling, and Kevin was sure he was just waiting for him to open his locker. Kevin was getting tired of having the door slammed every time he spun the combination. He could almost hear the metallic clang vibrating in his ears before he got the door open.

But it seemed like a different guy every time, and Kevin couldn't figure out how to tell some total stranger to leave him alone before the kid had even done anything. And afterward Kevin was left standing there with a slammed locker and a hot, heavy feeling inside. The kids always shrugged comically, as if it was all just an accident. How could you start a fight over an accident?

Kevin could hear the buses revving their engines and pulling out of the parking lot. He was trying to decide if it would do any good to just stand there and stare at his locker until the last bus left and the hall cleared. He had brought his bike to school that day because he was planning to stay late, but the kid might have to leave in order to catch his own bus. In the long run, it probably wouldn't matter. If he found a way around this hassle, the Hadley kids would only think of some other way to get him. At least this was predictable.

"Hey, Kevin, how's it going?"

The voice sounded unexpectedly friendly.

Kevin looked around fast and saw Andy hurrying toward him down the row of lockers. Out of the corner of his eye he saw the other kid straighten up and jam his hands in his rear jeans pockets. Before he headed off in the opposite direction, he flashed Kevin a brief grin and a wink. Kevin wondered suddenly if he'd made more of it than there really was. The guys who kept bugging him, they all looked like this guy—grubby and bored. Maybe hassling Kevin wasn't a big deal to anyone except Charley. Maybe it was just a way to pass the time and get a few laughs. If somebody new came along, maybe they'd forget about him. It was a startling thought.

"Okay, I guess," Kevin said to Andy. He turned back to his locker and spun the combination, wishing somebody new would come along soon. "How about you?"

"Good," Andy said. "I hear you're acing Mr. Fowler's geometry class."

Kevin felt his face flush. The last thing he wanted was to stand out for anything, even math. If his new theory was right, the less the Hadley kids noticed him, the better. So why was he going to spend the next couple of hours hanging around the school waiting for the Dungeons & Dragons Club meeting to be over so he could talk to Charley? Kevin wasn't sure he understood that one himself.

"Hey, that's a real compliment from Fowler," Andy said. "Don't get hot under the collar about it. He was wondering if you'd be interested in joining the Math Club and trying out for the Math Team. He said you're better at geometry already than some of the kids he's been teaching all year."

That was what Kevin had been dreaming about earlier, doing the things he'd done at Fort Carson, being on the Math Team and playing Dungeons & Dragons. But now that he had the chance, he wasn't sure it was such a good idea.

"Thanks, Andy, but I don't think anybody wants me joining anything around here."

Kevin tossed a couple of notebooks in his locker and pulled out his math book and his biology book. He figured he had time to do some homework while Charley was in the Dungeons & Dragons meeting.

"Look, if you're still thinking about Charley, don't," Andy said bluntly. "She's not into math, and I don't think any of those other jerks even know what Math Club is." Andy grinned at Kevin's look of surprise. "Yeah, I've seen them hassling you. They always do that to new kids—it's just been more fun with you because you're Army. You've been keeping your cool—that's the best way to make them stop."

"Yeah?" Kevin stared at his locker and shook his head.

"I wish somebody'd tell them the sideshow's ready to call it quits."

Andy laughed. "Look—about the Math Team. All the kids care about is making the team work. You know, we beat teams in Scottsburg and Orleans last semester. If we can up the team average we could seriously compete with some of the Indianapolis teams. Fowler thinks you could help us. I think that's all anybody on the team is going to care about."

Kevin thought about it. Maybe Andy was right. Maybe this was a chance to start all over in Hadley. He could talk to Charley this afternoon, square things away with her, and join the Math Club. He could make the team, he was sure of that.

"Well, what do you say?" Andy asked him.

Kevin slammed his locker shut and grinned at Andy. "I say, when's the next meeting?"

"All right! Thursday after school, Fowler's homeroom." Andy checked his watch. "Look—I've got to run. I'm late for D&D as it is, but I wanted to talk to you."

Kevin waved him on. "Go on, nobody can get anywhere without the Dungeon Master. And I don't need Charley blaming me for anything else!"

Andy laughed. "Okay. I'll see you Thursday afternoon, then."

"Count on it."

Kevin breezed through his biology homework and settled in to his math problems. He liked the careful logic of geometry, the detailed proofs. He especially loved the unreality of it all. You started with a point that wasn't there, then you connected it to a second point that wasn't there, and you had a line that wasn't there. Add another point and you could make two more lines and a triangle that wasn't there, all starting from one imaginary point.

He had nearly finished the page of proofs when he heard the kids coming down the hall from the Dungeons & Dragons meeting. He folded his paper into the book, shoved it inside his backpack, and stood up quickly. He was hoping he could catch Charley alone.

She was talking to two other girls, the three of them laughing together.

"When Ernie's dwarf tried to climb that cliff and slid down into the swamp, I thought I was going to die laughing," one girl said.

"Ernie tried everything he could think of," the other one said. "He got Alan's wizard to try his Feather Fall spell—"

"And when that failed, he tried a saving throw." The first girl groaned. "One dwarf buried up to his neck in the swamp."

Charley shook her head. "Ernie should have known better in the first place. Dwarves are lousy climbers. He should have let a couple of thieves go up first and let down a rope."

"Need a ride, Charley?" the first girl asked.

"No, thanks," she said, running lightly down the steps

to the parking lot and dropping her books on the concrete ledge at the base of the stairway. "My mom's
picking me up. She should be here any minute."

"Okay, see you tomorrow." The girl waved and the
two of them went on out to the lot.

Kevin couldn't get his feet to move. He'd been waiting since last Friday at the library for the chance to talk
to Charley alone, and now he didn't think he could. His
mouth was dry and his books stuck to his palm. As he
watched, Charley hoisted herself up on the ledge. She
dusted off her hands and flipped her hair neatly back,
then sat there watching for her mother, drumming the
heels of her boots against the wall.

Do something, Kevin told himself. She'll drive up any
minute and Charley'll be gone. You're never going to
catch her alone again.

"Hi, Charley."

The words were out of his mouth before he realized
it. He knew it was him speaking because he heard his
voice crack. He winced, but the words got his feet
unstuck and he found himself walking down the steps
toward her.

Charley turned her head to answer. He could see the
friendly look on her face when she turned to see who it
was, and he saw it harden. Her eyes narrowed.

"What do you want, Army brat?" she demanded.

Kevin stopped a few feet from her. He dropped his
backpack on the ground and left his arms at his sides,
and tried to look as unthreatening as possible. He had an

idea that there was a better way of standing up to Charley than fighting her. "I went to the library," he started. "I read the newspapers."

"So?" Charley said. "Am I supposed to be impressed that you can read or something?"

"I read about the Proving Ground," Kevin went on. "What the government did was wrong, taking people's homes like that and not even paying them right away. And I read about your great-grandfather standing up to them. I'm sorry about him, Charley. I wanted you to know."

Charley glared at him. "I don't care what you say, Army brat. People like your father killed my great-grandfather, and they couldn't care less as long as they met their schedules and got their job done so the people in Washington were happy."

Kevin stiffened. "My father's not like that! He would never have gone along with something that's wrong!"

"Grow up, Army brat!" Charley laughed at him. "Your father is just one dirty cog in the great military machine and he does what he's told, like all the others."

"My name is Kevin," he told her slowly, "not Army brat. And my father does what he thinks is right. Anyway, your great-grandfather wasn't down on the Army— I read what he said—he was angry at the government bureaucracy, not the Army." He stopped himself and shook his head. If he kept on this way, she'd just think he wanted to argue with her, and he didn't.

"I wanted you to know that I understood why you

were so angry," he said finally. "I didn't want to argue with you again, okay?"

She turned away sharply and scanned the street. Kevin figured she was looking for her mother's car.

"It sounds like you had some excitement climbing cliffs this afternoon," he said, trying to get them on neutral ground.

Charley stared at the passing cars.

"It must have been fun trying to lay out the cliffs and the climbers on the game board," Kevin went on, "especially the swamp. I saw the models you had last time, they were super. Not like those little die-cast models they sell in the hobby stores—they looked like they were hand carved or something. I really liked them."

Charley didn't say anything for a minute, then her voice sounded almost unwilling. "They *are* hand carved. I made them."

"You did?" Kevin was astonished. "They were beautiful, Charley. That's a real talent."

She shrugged. "It's a gift. I'm trying to learn how to train it, but right now it's just a gift." She turned and stared narrowly at him. "I inherited it from my great-grandfather."

That's not all you got from him, Kevin said to himself. Aloud he said, "I mean it—I'm impressed, Charley. I've never seen carvings like that."

"Well, you've never seen my great-grandfather's work," she snapped. She slid down off the low wall and faced him, her hands on her hips.

"He used to carve things for the house," she said, talking rapidly, "animals sitting on the fireplace or beside a door, looking like they were ready to jump up when you came into the room. I've seen the pictures, and we still have some of them at home now. And he'd carve toys for his kids and his grandkids."

She advanced toward him, and Kevin felt his feet back up. Her eyes were locked on his and he couldn't make himself look away. Her words rushed on, like a flooded stream racing over a broken dam.

"Up to the end he carved things," Charley was saying, "beautiful things, not just little figures like I do but real art. He was carving when they forced him out of his house. He told his son he was working on a special gift for one of his grandsons, my father, and then he died. He said it was in the house somewhere, he said he was going to go back and get it after he won the case, and then your Army killed him and he never finished it."

Kevin felt the stair railing bump against his back. He wanted to interrupt her, to shut her up, to calm her down somehow. He had the strange feeling that she was hurting inside, and that's what made her so angry. He wished he knew how to make the hurt go away, but she kept coming toward him, and he pressed back against the iron railing, helpless and tongue-tied.

"We never even knew what it was because your Army wouldn't let anybody go back inside the house," Charley told him bitterly. "They packed up our stuff and they trucked it over to my grandfather and there was no surprise carving there. Some Army brat must have ended up playing with the gift my great-grandfather was making for my father, and the dumb kid probably didn't care about it and just threw it away. That's your Army for you, Mr. Kevin Army brat, and why don't you just go back inside your Proving Ground and leave me alone!"

The stair railing was digging sharply into his back. Kevin wanted to tell her that was terrible; he wanted to say he knew how she felt. But he couldn't say that to those blazing eyes and that furious face.

"That wasn't me!" he shouted, and she finally stood still, a few inches away from him. She was poised to fight, he was sure of it. Well, if she wanted a fight, he'd make sure she knew where he stood.

"You're not your great-grandfather and I'm not the Colonel who was in charge of the Proving Ground then! I may be stuck living in Hadley, but at least I'm not down on anybody who's different, like you are. You could take a few lessons in manners, you know. I'll bet you could even learn how to act like a Charlene if you tried, instead of picking fights and trying to be some sort of one-person vigilante upholding the one true faith! But right now you're just a rude brat yourself, Chuck, and I'm sorry I ever wasted my time trying to talk to you."

Kevin was keeping his eyes on her hands so he'd be ready to block her first blow. He didn't see the car drive up, but he heard the wheels screech to a stop.

"Hey, Charley, what gives?"

Charley stiffened. She backed away from Kevin, but

she didn't turn to look at the old, beat-up Buick sedan. "Nothing, Duane," she called back, her voice expressionless.

The guy she was talking to had already gotten out of the driver's seat. He smoothed one hand over his crew cut and walked slowly around the front of the car, his glossy black boots clicking ominously on the pavement. He glared at Kevin through narrowed eyes.

"Hey, kid," he said, "what do you think you're doing to my cousin?"

Kevin felt a flash of hot fear in his chest. He remembered the pounding Charley had given Chris, and Charley wasn't any bigger than he was. Her cousin was taller and heavier. Kevin was willing to bet the bulk in his chest and arms wasn't just padding in his winter jacket, either.

"Get lost, Duane," Charley said sharply. "He's just a dumb jerk who wanted to talk about my carvings."

"Isn't he the new Army kid?"

The voice came from inside the car.

Kevin darted a quick look at the front passenger seat and saw a heavy, flushed face hanging out the window. The face smiled, but the sharp black eyes stayed cold and the voice was taunting.

"Yeah, Duane," the passenger said, "he's the new officer's kid, the one that's living in your house."

Kevin wondered if he could outrun Duane if he cut through the bleachers in the football field. They couldn't chase him in the car, but could he make it over the fence if Duane tried to run after him? He could see Orion loping easily across the field, vaulting onto the fence, pulling himself over the top, dropping lightly to the ground on the other side. Kevin could also see himself tripping on the turf or catching his jeans on the top of the fence.

He kept his eyes on Duane and tried to think of a better way to escape. He was definitely not going to let this guy start a fight with him. He thought bitterly about his old dreams of being a hero like his father. That's all they were—dreams. It was well and good for Orion to draw his sword and ignore the odds, but this was a time for Kevin Spencer to remember his father's warning instead of his heroism. Kevin wasn't about to sail into this battle half-cocked. In the real world Kevin wasn't an Army officer or a Dungeons & Dragons ranger. He was just an ordinary kid facing a bully who hated everything about him, and he was pretty sure the odds were in the bully's favor.

Duane slowly took his hands out of his pockets. Kevin could see a senior ring glinting on one finger. Then he saw the cold afternoon sun catch something shiny hidden in the other hand.

"I'm glad to meet you, Kevin Spencer," Duane sneered. "I've been on the lookout for you. I always like to give our military friends in Hadley a proper welcome."

Duane flipped his hand and Kevin saw a six-inch blade snap out. Definitely the odds were in the other guy's favor. Kevin darted a quick look at Charley. She was standing beside the ledge, clutching her books against her chest, staring down at the pavement. She looked up and her eyes met Kevin's briefly, then she turned her head to look down toward the main entrance of the school building.

"I hate to break up your welcoming committee's reception," she said coldly, "but Mr. Harris and Mr. Green are on their way to their cars. I think Chess Club and French Club are over."

Duane kept staring at Kevin, a twisted smile on his face. "You're a little too young to be driving, aren't you, Spencer? But I'll bet your father has a car, a nice car with neat little military stickers on it. You tell him to be careful where he parks it, won't you? You see, I'm always on the lookout for military cars around town."

He moved one finger slightly and the blade disappeared.

"One more thing, Spencer—you keep away from my cousin, got that?" The smile disappeared completely from Duane's face. "I don't like her being bothered by Army scum."

He turned and strolled back toward his car, pausing beside Charley. She jerked away from him as he reached out to pat her shoulder. Kevin felt a sudden hot flush of anger in his chest, an anger he hadn't felt when Duane was threatening him.

But Duane only laughed at Charley's flinch. He opened the driver's door and stared back at Kevin over the roof of the car.

"Remember to give your father my advice about the

car, okay, kid? Hadley is a nice, clean town. We don't like people coming in and messing it up with Army trash."

The heat of anger died away. Kevin wondered how somebody who looked like a Marine sergeant, with his spit-shined boots and crisp haircut, could hate the military so much.

The other guy in the front seat snorted.

"Great words, man," he said loudly, as though he meant Kevin to hear. "You talk big, Duane, but I'm waiting to see you do something."

"Shut up, Pete," Charley told him.

Pete laughed. "That's right, Duane—that pretty knife of yours isn't enough protection—you need your baby cousin too!"

"Both of you shut up," Duane said sharply. He revved the engine. "You just wait, Pete, and see who's the big talker. I got it all planned out."

"Sure you do," Pete said, and laughed again.

Duane glared through the windshield at Kevin. "As for you, Spencer," he called out, "I'll get you out of Hadley, you and all the rest of the Army scumbags. Give it a month." Then he popped the clutch. The Buick bucked, then it jumped and roared out of the parking lot.

Kevin carefully stepped away from the stair railing. He could still feel it engraved in his back.

"I'm sorry about that," Charley said suddenly, her voice dragging and unwilling. "Duane—there's some-

thing wrong with him. And with Pete egging him on—"
She shook her head. "You'll keep away from them if
you're smart."

"Thanks for standing up for me," Kevin said, his voice
rusty, but meaning it.

Charley shrugged. "You stood up for yourself. Most
kids run when they see him."

"I guess I didn't know enough to run," Kevin said
unsteadily. Her saying he'd stood up to Duane felt good,
but he knew inside that he hadn't, any more than he'd
really stood up to the kids who were hassling him at
school. All he'd really done was keep his cool, like Andy
had said. Kevin remembered Duane's knife. How long
would staying cool be enough? He had the feeling that
the time was going to come when he'd have to stand up
for himself for real.

Charley was still staring out at the parking lot.
"There's my mother now. I wish she'd been here when
he was—I've tried to tell her about Duane, but she
doesn't want to listen. And his parents don't have the
first idea of how to deal with him. They try to pretend
this is just some sort of phase he's going through—they
say he'll outgrow it like a little kid quits playing cops and
robbers." She gave a sharp laugh. "They just won't admit
that switchblades are a lot more dangerous than cap
guns!"

Then she ran toward her mother's car and climbed
into the passenger seat without a backward glance.

Kevin picked up his backpack and started to walk

around to his bike at the front of the building, but his books weighed a ton and his legs wobbled and he couldn't seem to find a comfortable stride. When he finally reached his bike, his hands shook so hard he had to try the combination three times before the lock clicked open. He slid the chain out awkwardly and wound it under the seat. Then he leaned against the bike stand and tried to find a way to breathe evenly again.

Had he really been going to challenge Duane? Was he crazy? But it had felt right when Duane had reached for Charley. Then he remembered what Duane had said about his father's car. What did he do to cars with military stickers? Kevin could still see that switchblade, and the glint off the steel made him feel sick. He glanced down at his bike tires, half expecting to see that they were slashed.

He could hear Duane's angry voice in his ears again, and the other guy's mocking taunts. What was it Duane had planned out? What was going to happen in the next month? Kevin didn't want to imagine. Charley had said there was something wrong with Duane, and Kevin believed her.

"I want to go home," he whispered to himself, but he couldn't think of a home to run to. His mother had a cross-stitch wall hanging that said, Home Is Where the Army Sends You, but the Army had sent them to Hadley.

≡ 5 ≡
NOBODY LIKES A PEACEMAKER

When Kevin thought he could ride his bicycle without losing his balance, he swung it out of the rack and down the driveway to the street. He pedaled slowly at first, concentrating on the uneven pavement and the traffic. He didn't want to think about Duane Hanson or Hadley, or the threatening weight that seemed to hang over him. But he couldn't quite keep from thinking about Charley.

He kept seeing Charley standing in front of the parking lot ledge, clutching her books, staring at the ground. She hadn't liked what her cousin was doing. She hadn't liked her cousin. She said there was something wrong with him. Personally, Kevin thought Duane was more than a little crazy. Kevin grinned faintly at the thought of Charley telling Duane to leave him alone. He guessed she would have been only too happy to beat him up herself, but she didn't like Duane baiting him like that.

Then his grin faded. Kevin couldn't forget the icy

green look of hatred in Charley's eyes when she told him about her great-grandfather's carvings.

"Go ahead and hate me, Chuck," he muttered into the chill wind. He told himself she'd find out she was wrong one of these days, and then she could hate herself for it.

The funny thing was that Kevin thought Charley really would be angry with herself if she ever found out she was wrong. She was all full of this holier-than-thou righteousness—it was all right for her to hate Kevin and run him out of the Dungeons & Dragons Club and want to bash him in a fair fight, but she didn't like the idea of her cousin taunting him with a switchblade. If she ever figured out she was wrong about hating the Army, she'd collapse like an abandoned pile of empty clothes.

That's it! Kevin realized. He swung with the light onto the long street leading toward the Proving Ground entrance and laughed out loud, wondering why he hadn't thought of it when she first told him.

"I'll *show* her she doesn't know the first thing about me!" he shouted into the wind as he pedaled faster. He would find the carving her great-grandfather had been working on, and he'd give it back to her.

Kevin could just see her face, the astonishment on it, the green eyes widening as he held it out to her. He could see the dark flush spreading up from her neck to the roots of her flaming hair. She'd be in such shock she wouldn't be able to find words for him.

No, scratch that, Kevin thought as he shifted gears on the bumpy gravel shoulder. He couldn't imagine Charley at a loss for words. Maybe she'd stumble over herself apologizing to him, thanking him for finding the carving. Maybe she'd actually call him Kevin. Maybe she'd open her eyes and actually see him, not just some enemy she'd made up, but a real person, a guy she ought to like.

And then he'd turn around and walk away and never speak to her again.

But Kevin didn't think he could do that. What he really wished was that he could find the carving and give it back to her and just wipe out all those years between when her great-grandfather died and now, so that she'd meet him and get to know him and like him for himself, not even thinking about his father's job. It occurred to Kevin that he didn't have any idea what Charley's father did, and he didn't care.

Kevin checked the sparse traffic and eased his bike up onto the paved road, where the going was easier. The dry, weathered stalks of corn flew past him, rustling paper soft in the breeze. Kevin knew most of the farmers only worked the land part time. They had jobs in town that brought in a regular income. A lot of them worked on the Proving Ground, in fact. But it must still be hard for them to have a crop fail because of a drought.

He reached the southeast corner of the Proving Ground, and the security fence started up beside him. Through the wire he could see the stark trees and the dry, tangled undergrowth. Kevin shook his head. The land the Proving Ground was built on certainly wasn't any better than the farmland still surrounding it. In fact, it was worse. Despite last year's drought, there were big marshy patches that stretched off to the north, where nothing but weeds could grow, and plenty of dry, uneven land that couldn't have ever been much use for crops. But Kevin didn't think it mattered whether the Government had taken rich land or poor land—the people of Hadley resented the taking. They probably looked at their water-starved corn and said that if they were still on their old land, they'd have something to harvest after all. The reality of the situation wouldn't make any difference to them.

Kevin told himself firmly to stop thinking about Hadley people and how they felt. He wasn't going to be able to change their opinions anyhow. The only one he could maybe hope to reach was Charley, and only then if he could find her great-grandfather's carving.

The question was where. Where could he look? The carving had to be hidden someplace where no kid living there since would have found it, someplace the builders wouldn't have found it when they split the house into pieces and transported it to the circle of houses that would become the Housing Area for the military personnel. Kevin mentally wandered through the house.

The basement couldn't count, because they would have dug that new when they moved the house there. There were plenty of closets and cupboards in the house, but they were too obvious. Anything hidden there would have been found right away. There was that peculiar narrow walkway at the top of the stairs. It seemed to lead nowhere except to a window in the far wall. Kevin pictured the stairs coming up from the entrance hall, curving around to lead to the bedrooms. Along the side of the bathroom that odd little hall stretched to a single window. That could be promising.

Kevin sighed. If it led to nothing but a window, there probably wasn't anyplace to hide anything. But it was worth checking out. He considered other possibilities. An attic would be a great hiding place, but there didn't seem to be much of an attic—it was more like a crawl space. There was a huge attic fan that they could switch on in the summer, although Kevin doubted they'd ever use it. He'd turned it on once to see what it did, and the roar was deafening. But there must be some sort of space up there for them to have put the fan in. Could it have been a real attic originally? Kevin wondered if there was any way he could get up there and look around.

Kevin glanced over at the Proving Ground. Through the fence he saw two deer grazing beside the trees, oblivious to the occasional car roaring down the road. He coasted, watching them nuzzle the ground for bits of grass. Right then Kevin felt an overwhelming desire for a friend to be biking with him, a friend he could tell to look at the deer and share the moment with, a friend he could discuss plans for searching the house with. But there was no whirring sound of a second bike in the road alongside his.

Then the mood was broken. One of the deer looked up suddenly, shreds of grass still caught in its mouth. It looked around, its ears pivoting like radar scanning its surroundings, its nostrils quivering. The other deer looked up also, still chewing slowly. Then their tails flicked up white and both deer bounded into the trees.

Kevin couldn't figure out what had startled them. He hadn't noticed any sudden noise or seen any movement anywhere. Then he caught a faint whiff of smoke and sat up straighter on his bike. No one would be cooking out this time of year, and autumn leaves must have long since been raked and burned. Where could the smoke be coming from?

Looking up, Kevin saw a gray cloud hovering over the Proving Ground. He pedaled harder and caught up with it. He could smell the smoke clearly, now that he could see it. On the other side of the fence a fire burned jaggedly, consuming the dry, brown grass and thick vines and bushes. It was a ground fire, blown steadily southwest by the low wind. Kevin wondered how it could have started, and shifted gears to get more speed. He'd better report it as soon as he reached the security guard at the front gate.

As he bent over the handlebars, a gust of wind sent a burning twig skittering through the fence and onto the road. The flame died out as Kevin watched, but it would be so easy for a twig like that to land in a clump of dry grass and start a serious fire right beside the road. Burning bits might even jump the road and sail into the farms on the other side. He looked at the drought-stricken corn whispering in the fields. Kevin imagined the weathered gray stalks with flaming heads as the fire marched from farm to farm.

He skidded to a stop inside the gate and automatically pulled out his ID as the guard glanced up from his book and waved him through.

"Hey," Kevin called to him. "There's a fire in the Proving Ground, between here and the south fence."

"What?" The guard put down his book, slowly got to his feet, and walked over to frown at Kevin. "What is it, kid?"

Kevin pointed. "There's a fire in the Proving Ground—"

The guard sighed. "Sure there is. They're burning the undergrowth. They do that on days like this when it's not too windy. Otherwise it grows too thick, and maybe the rounds they shoot off could start a fire that's not under control. It's no big deal."

"That was under control?" Kevin asked. "I saw flaming twigs fly through the fence. It's dangerous!"

"Did your flaming twigs start any fires?" the guard asked him.

"No, but—"

"So it wasn't dangerous, was it?" The guard shook his head. "Where do you get off, waltzing in here and thinking you know better than everybody else, huh? We've been here a long time, kid. We know what's safe and what isn't. So go on home and don't worry, okay?"

Kevin stood open-mouthed, one foot on the ground, the other poised on a pedal. Not dangerous? What did this jerk think dangerous was?

Grimly, Kevin reminded himself that security was important, even if this guard was an idiot. It wouldn't do any good in the long run to tell the guard off. He made himself close his mouth and stamped down on the pedal, and his bike leaped down the road. Everyone in Hadley was crazy! They all knew better than any newcomer ever could, no matter how stupid they were. Did they think something was right just because it had always been done that way? What did they think progress was, anyhow? Probably just something that got in their way if they let it.

Kevin shifted gears until he was flying. Go ahead, he thought, burn down the farms. See if I care! But he did. He cared about the waste. And he cared about the people who might get hurt if all those idiots who insisted they'd always done it that way were wrong.

He cut across the circle around Building 100, where his father's office was, and headed down the road to the Housing Area. He coasted into his driveway and swung off his bike to open the garage door.

"Still trying to get in the Dungeons & Dragons Club?"

Kevin jumped at the unexpected voice. He turned around and saw Chris standing in the grass beside his driveway, a basketball under one arm. A fading bruise was still visible along one cheekbone.

"Hi," Kevin said, and raised the creaking garage door.

"I thought Charley didn't want you in the club," Chris said.

Kevin set the bike on its kickstand instead of wheeling it into the garage and turned around to face Chris.

"That's right," he said.

"So why are you staying late when the Dungeons & Dragons Club is meeting?"

Kevin frowned at him. "I had some stuff to take care of. What does it matter to you, anyway?"

Chris shrugged and bounced the ball. "I just wondered. Want to shoot some baskets?"

"No, thanks." Kevin felt angry inside. Duane threatening him, the guard telling him he knew best, and now Chris keeping an eye on what he was doing, making sure it was what *he* thought Army kids should do.

"And for your information I'm joining the Math Club," Kevin told him sharply. "I'll make the Math Team too, probably."

Chris caught the ball and held it, staring at Kevin. "I thought I told you Army kids don't join school things in Hadley."

"Well, I guess you're wrong," Kevin said. Sorry, Dad, he mentally told his father. This is one military kid I just can't get along with, even for you.

Chris shook his head. "I don't get it. What is it with you and your father, anyway? Both of you coming here and trying to shake things up."

"What do you mean?" Kevin asked, surprised at the sudden shift in Chris's focus.

"Your father's trying to change the way things work

around here," Chris said. "But he's wasting his time. Everybody knows green-suiters come and go, but the civilians run things on the Proving Ground. The key to getting by is to just let things move along at their own pace and not make waves, but your father keeps trying to stir things up. He's even making trouble for the other Army guys here, like my dad. And you're just as bad, trying to get in good with the town kids and join their clubs!"

"What are you talking about?" Kevin demanded, thoroughly confused. "The Army runs things here, not the civilians. They work for my father. They're supposed to do what he says, like he does what his boss tells him."

"Well, I've got news for you," Chris told him. "Even the Colonel on post has been telling your father to cool it. The Colonel's going for his General's star, and he doesn't want anybody messing things up for him. Your father's making trouble for everybody, and they're not going to stand for it. You better tell him that, too."

"I don't tell my father how to do his job," Kevin said, feeling a little frightened. This was the second threat that afternoon that he was supposed to pass on to his father.

"Somebody better," Chris said, "or he's going to find himself in real trouble. And you better start playing by the rules too. Army kids stay with Army kids in Hadley, and town kids stay with town kids. Got it?"

Kevin kicked up the stand on his bike and wheeled it into the garage, propping it against the side so his father would have room to pull the car in. He came out and eased the garage door down, then dusted off his hands. The lump of fear that had started to grow in his stomach had turned into an icy anger raging in his chest. He was utterly sick of everybody in Hadley telling him what to do and what to think.

"Thanks for the advice, Chris," he said coolly. "Keep your eye on the Math Team results, because you'll be seeing my name there."

Chris bounced the ball again, watching it kick up dust each time it hit the driveway. "Don't be stupid, Kevin," he warned.

Kevin turned away from him and headed to the front stairs, listening to the crack of the basketball on the cold pavement.

"Give your father the message," Chris called to him as he climbed up to the front porch.

Kevin stood a moment before opening the front door. He wanted to tell Chris to keep his threats to himself, to tell him what a jerk he was. He wanted to tell Chris Waverly that he was just as bad as Duane Hanson and he hated him. But he could just see Chris telling his dad he got in a fight with LTC Spencer's kid. It would be more trouble for his own father. And it sounded like his father was having as much trouble at work as Kevin was having at school. It was better to just keep his mouth shut.

"Don't say I didn't warn you," Chris said finally, and then the bouncing of the ball got fainter. When Kevin finally allowed himself to turn around and look, Chris was dribbling the ball down the road to his own house.

Kevin took a deep breath and steeled himself to go inside. He didn't want to think about Chris's veiled threats or Duane's blunt ones. He wanted to concentrate on a problem he could actually do something about.

"I'll find it," he vowed to himself as he pushed the door open. He would find the carving and show Charley she was wrong about him. And if he could make one person change her mind about him, maybe the others would too.

But as he climbed the stairs to his room, Kevin felt a weight in his chest telling him it wouldn't be that easy.

≡6≡

AN OLD GRUDGE

"**Y**ou going to the Winter Art Fair this weekend?" Andy asked as they walked down the hall after Math Club.

Kevin shook his head. "My folks are, but I think I'll pass. You're supposed to go to art fairs when it's warm, not when it's thirty-five degrees and windy out."

Andy laughed and pushed his glasses up on his nose. "You couldn't have an ice sculpture contest in the summer," he pointed out. "It's warmer than usual, actually. The sculptures will probably melt before the fair's over this year. I've heard of years when the sculptures stood until April."

Kevin shuddered. "Way too cold for me. Anyhow, that's probably just another Hadley myth."

"Probably," Andy agreed. "But the whole town will be down there, checking out the ice sculptures and the craft booths. A lot of tourists come in for the fair too. Downtown streets will be curb-to-curb solid people."

"Yeah, *frozen* solid," Kevin said.

"Well, Eric and Jack and I are going," Andy said. "Give me a call if you change your mind."

"I'll think about it," Kevin told him. He felt a glad twinge at being included.

Eric and Jack were in the Math Club too. Eric's dad was with Arvin Industries, and Jack's dad worked at the Dow Corning offices in nearby Asherton. The four boys had started hanging around together on the weekends, and Kevin found himself unwinding. He thought sometimes that his first couple of weeks as a Hadley freshman had moved in slow motion, or been a series of black-and-white snapshots frozen in an album with empty white pages between the moments.

The action had slowly come up to speed as Kevin and the Hadley hardliners had made an uneasy truce and agreed to ignore each other. None of the kids who'd bugged him in the beginning ever came up to congratulate him about making the Math Team, but most of the harassment had faded away. Kevin stood in line for lunch with Andy or Eric or Jack, and nobody tried to elbow the group of them to the back. And in math class he was no longer sitting in the back corner. He'd moved up to the front row after making the team, and somehow nobody slid into the seat just as he got to it.

Kevin still got his locker slammed every now and then, but he'd decided it was just something to do when a guy got bored and couldn't think of a better way to have some fun. Kevin shrugged it off and forgot about it as soon as he respun the combination and pulled his locker open. He had too much else to think about these days.

Between Math Club and schoolwork and new friends, it finally seemed like his life was moving along normally. Kevin hadn't forgotten the vision of Duane with his switchblade or the sound of Chris bouncing his basketball, but he didn't think too much about either of them, and he'd never given his father their warnings. Kevin suspected his father had enough to worry about—he still came home tense and short tempered in the evening, snapping orders like Kevin and his mom were troops in the field, then apologizing. Kevin spent most of his time in his room and tried not to think about his father's troubles at the Proving Ground.

He kept thinking a lot about Charley, though. He would see her in the halls at school and come up with good things to say to her in his mind, but he hadn't talked to her since the day she had told him about her great-grandfather. He kept imagining how he would walk up to her one afternoon and tell her he was looking for the carving, but somehow he could never think of the right words. And she was always in a crowd, anyway. So he hung around with Andy and Eric and Jack, and talked math, and tried to ignore the Hansons.

"Sure I can't talk you into it?" Andy asked once more as they stopped by his locker. He twirled the scuffed dial on the combination, tossed in a couple of math books with a dull clang, and pulled out his German text.

"Positive," Kevin said, and then a thought flared in the back of his mind. "Unless—who enters the ice sculpture contest, anyway?"

Andy shrugged and slammed his locker shut. "Anybody who wants to, I guess. Not me. How come?"

"Just wondering." Was ice sculpture anything like wood carving? If it was, Kevin thought Charley might enter.

He followed Andy down a deserted side hall to the back parking lot exit. They passed the darkened metal-shop room, but Kevin saw there were lights on in the wood shop. About half a dozen kids were inside, scattered at different worktables under the harsh fluorescent lights.

Charley was sitting at one of the high tables near the door, perched on a metal stool. Her long red hair was tied back with a black ribbon and a dark smock covered her clothes. She was speckled with wood dust, and pale wood chips clung to the smock. She was working on a carving with a vibrating sander, the center of an enthusiastic eruption of wood dust.

Without stopping to think, Kevin shoved open the door and waved at Charley.

"Hi!" he called over the buzz of the sander.

She switched it off and looked up in surprise through a pair of plastic protective goggles, then frowned when she saw who it was. She stole a quick look behind her to see if anybody else had noticed, then dropped the sander on her workbench, slid off her stool, and strode to the doorway.

"I was wondering if you were entering the ice sculpture contest this weekend," Kevin said quickly.

"What?" Charley bit the word off, stepping into the hall and jerking the door shut behind her.

"The ice sculpture contest at the Winter Art Fair," Kevin said, gesturing at the wood carving she'd been working on. "You know—wood, ice—I thought if you were good at one, you might be good at the other, too."

Charley glanced up and down the hall, but Andy had disappeared. She turned back to stare at Kevin as though he'd lost his mind.

"About the other carving," Kevin went on, "I just wanted you to know—I'm looking for it. If it's still anywhere in the house, I'll find it. And I'll get it back to you."

"What are you talking about?" Charley asked sharply. She ripped off her goggles and twirled them on her finger. A fine shower of wood dust spattered across the floor around her. A few strands of fiery hair had escaped and hung down across one cheek. She looked impatient and irritated, and beautiful.

But Kevin felt confused. He'd thought she'd be pleased to know he was looking for the carving.

"Your great-grandfather's carving," he told her. "It's got to be in the house somewhere—I can't believe anybody would have stolen it. It's somewhere nobody thought to look, and I'm going to find it for you."

Charley's face eased into surprise.

Kevin grinned at her. "Anyway, I saw you here, and Andy was just telling me about the ice sculpture contest, and I wondered if you'd be entering." He paused a second, then went on. "I wasn't going to go to the Art Fair, but if you're entering, I thought I might go see what you can do."

Charley began to laugh and shook her head slowly. "You've got to be eighteen to enter, you turkey. I thought you were making fun of me."

"I wasn't—I didn't know," he stammered, feeling stupid. "That it was only for adults, I mean. I thought you'd be good at it, that's all."

"Obviously," she said, still chuckling a little. She caught the loose hair and tucked it behind her ear.

"And anyway," he told her, "I thought you'd want to know about the other."

She stopped chuckling. "You won't find it," she said flatly.

Kevin shrugged. "Don't be so sure—I might surprise you."

Charley stared at him, her green eyes sharp and speculative. "I don't know what to make of you, Army brat," she said, but there was no real malice in the nickname this time. "Maybe you *will* surprise me."

She glanced behind her at the shop room. "Gotta go," she said abruptly, and disappeared into the wood shop, slamming the door behind her and leaving a flurry of little wood flecks dancing in the air.

Kevin wandered along the hallway, smiling to himself. Andy was waiting for him past the doorway, one hand over his mouth, trying to hold in his laughter.

"You could have told me it was only for adults!" Kevin said, aiming a mock punch at Andy's stomach.

"No, I couldn't." Andy shook his head. He was leaning up against the wall, laughing helplessly now. "I didn't know."

"Stop laughing!" Kevin said, then burst out laughing himself.

Andy shook his head, still chuckling. "Man, you have got it bad for that girl! I thought you'd made up your mind to steer clear of her."

"I'm just trying to clear the air," Kevin protested.

"Tell me another," Andy said, snorting. "You better wise up, Kevin. Charley may be a great girl, but she's a Hanson."

"Let's talk trig," Kevin said.

Andy reached out and caught Kevin's coat sleeve. He wasn't laughing any longer. "I'm serious, man—I don't care how hot you think she is, you get involved with the girl, you get involved with the family. And her crazy cousin is bad news."

Kevin stared past his friend, remembering the sunlight running off Duane Hanson's knife blade. "I've met him," he admitted, and told Andy about the run-in in the parking lot.

"Then you know what I mean," Andy said impatiently. "The Hansons do *not* just forgive and forget—once you cross them, they lie in wait until they can get back at you. Didn't Eric ever tell you what happened when his family moved here?"

Kevin fidgeted with the shoulder straps of his backpack and shook his head unwillingly. He didn't think he wanted to hear this.

"Eric's dad was in the Navy for six years, and his mom is Civil Service," Andy told him. "After Mr. Singer retired from the Navy, Mrs. Singer got offered some sort of promotion if they'd move to Hadley so she could work at the Proving Ground."

Kevin groaned—not the Proving Ground again. Why did everything in Hadley come back to the Proving Ground sooner or later?

Andy went on. "So they moved here, and Eric's dad got a job with Arvin. They bought a place out in the country, and they thought Hadley was a pretty nice town. Then the trouble started. Mrs. Singer started getting cold-shouldered at work for taking a job the people in town said somebody from Hadley should have gotten, then the Singers started having trouble at the house."

Kevin felt a flicker of curiosity. Eric had never said anything about this. But then, Eric didn't talk much except about math. "What trouble?" he asked.

"The neighbors. One afternoon Eric climbs off the school bus, pulls open the mailbox, and a dead rabbit falls out. Another day there's mud in their newspaper box, then it was broken eggs."

"But why?" Kevin asked.

Andy smiled, but it wasn't his usual open smile. It was flat and cold and unfriendly. "Guess who owned the property next door to the Singers' house?"

"Who?" Kevin demanded.

Andy smiled that chilly smile again. "Hansons, of course. Not Charley's father—her uncle."

"Uncle?" Kevin said uncertainly.

"Yeah. Duane Hanson's father."

Kevin stared. He couldn't think of anything to say.

"Duane Hanson's mother had an application in for a job at the Proving Ground," Andy went on. "She got turned down, and then Eric's mom was brought in. And Duane's got a chip on his shoulder a mile high anyway. You heard what he does with cars that have military stickers? Parks real close to them and slams his door into the other car's sidewall. Or gouges across the finish with something sharp. Puts his mark on them, one way or another."

"Yeah," Kevin said. "Duane told me to let my dad know he'd be on the lookout for our car."

Andy shook his head. "Believe him. You should have seen the Singers' car when Duane was finished with it. Of course, nobody ever admitted they saw Duane do anything, but word was all over school that Duane had done it again. Eric said his parents complained to the Hansons, but they insisted their son was a real straight arrow."

Kevin nodded. "Charley said she'd tried to tell her mom about Duane, but that the grown-ups wouldn't admit there was anything dangerous about him."

"That's the Hansons," Andy agreed. "They only see what they want, and they sure don't see Duane the way he is. Probably Mrs. Hanson wasn't qualified for the job Eric's mom got—but they didn't see that, either. They said it was outsiders causing trouble, like it was Eric's family's fault for moving to Hadley. And Duane was smart enough to stop bugging the Singers and start hassling somebody else."

"This is crazy!" Kevin exploded. "These people are crazy!"

"Hansons are losers," Andy said simply. "They can't seem to get ahead. And every time they screw up, they blame it all on the Proving Ground stealing their home and destroying their lives."

Kevin thought of Charley's carvings, but he kept quiet. He had the feeling Charley was going to be one Hanson who would end up successful, but he wondered if she'd have to get out of Hadley to do it.

"What is it with Hadley?" he burst out. "It's like the town's this closed-in little world rotting in on itself, but it doesn't want anybody to come in and shake things up and start anything getting better."

Andy shrugged. "Don't ask me. I understand how they must have felt back in 1940—a lot of people, especially the Hansons, got a bad shake from the government. But 1940 was a *long* time ago. Most people got over it. Not the Hansons, though—they carry the chips on their shoulders like that's all they are, somebody who got screwed by the government, and they don't ever *want* to be anything else."

"Yeah," Kevin nodded. "And they don't ever want anyone else to forget it, either." He swore suddenly. "Maybe it's time somebody made them forget it!"

"Are you asking for trouble?" Andy demanded.

"Didn't you have enough of that when you first got here?" He stopped at the exit door and grabbed Kevin's coat collar and shook him slightly. "Use some common sense! You already had one run-in with Duane Hanson, right? Well, that's nothing compared to what he'll do if you put the make on his cousin!"

Kevin groaned, irritated by his friend's caution. "I hear you—but I'm getting sick of watching my back for the Hansons! I know Duane's crazy, but Charley's not, and I'm not about to let him scare me away from her!"

≡ 7 ≡

ROTTEN TO THE CORE

Saturday morning, while his parents were planning their assault on the Winter Art Fair, Kevin laid his plans for exploring the house. He made a list of walls that might be hollow and spaces around closets that didn't seem to match the dimensions. There wasn't much more he could do as long as his parents hung around.

Go, go! he urged silently, frustrated at having to keep quiet. But they'd ask questions if they noticed him up to something unusual, questions Kevin didn't want to answer. If he found the carving and gave it to Charley, if he changed her way of thinking about the Army, it would be a good surprise for them. But if he didn't find it, he didn't want his parents to know what had been going on in school. It would just be one more thing for them to worry about.

So he killed time crawling around quietly, trying to squeeze his fingers into the cracks around uneven floorboards and pry them up, and checking for loose molding along the base of the walls. Everything seemed depressingly solid.

They're going to leave any minute, Kevin promised himself for the twentieth time, but he could still hear their voices rise and fall downstairs in the dining room. Finally he slipped out of his room and crossed quietly to the top of the stairs, where he could hear them more clearly. Since they had come to Hadley, his parents had spent a lot more time having soft discussions that would stop the moment he came into the room. He paused, out of sight, and concentrated on the low voices.

"—ammo was firing out into the air," his father was saying. "They weren't even pretending it was going through the chronographs. When I asked them what sort of test results they thought they'd get that way, they looked at each other, then one of them got this silly grin and said Gee, somebody must have just knocked something a little out of kilter a minute or so ago, all the earlier results were just fine. He even had a nice list of 'measurements' that proved the lot of ammunition was all right—measurements that he'd simply typed into the printer so it looked like he'd gotten readouts from the chronographs."

"Did you tell the Colonel?" Mrs. Spencer asked.

LTC Spencer swore. "Of course I told the Colonel— and he held up the list of 'measurements' and told me not to be so hard core. He said probably someone *had* just misset something right before I came in, but the data they'd already gotten was good, so why didn't I just sign it off and not worry about it."

"What do you mean?" Kevin thought his mother sounded frightened.

"I mean the Colonel doesn't want to make waves," his father snapped, "nothing that might rock his promotion. He wanted me to okay the test results even though I believed they were bull." LTC Spencer laughed, and it wasn't a pleasant sound. "And with my signature on the test, if the ammo turned out to be bad, it wouldn't be the Colonel's head that would roll. It would be mine."

There was silence. Kevin gripped the banister. What was going on in Hadley? What were these people thinking? How could they justify falsifying test reports? And what was this Colonel thinking to let those jerks go on cheating the Army and then try to use another officer to cover that cheating? He was as bad as they were— worse, because he didn't even have a grudge like the Hansons did to use as an excuse.

"What are you going to do?" Kevin's mother was saying.

"I can't sign the report," his father said shortly. "It may be peacetime, but if that ammo is bad and goes to some training camp and some kid gets killed—" His voice broke off.

"We don't have to go today," Kevin's mother said into the heavy silence. "I can understand your not wanting to mix with these people if you don't have to."

"No." LTC Spencer sighed. "This Winter Art Fair seems to be one of the few attractions Hadley has to offer. We might as well try to enjoy something here, at least. Anyway, maybe it'll do some good if these people see me out supporting the community instead of just coming down hard on them at the Proving Ground. And some of them actually do work—I'd like them to see us out in a social setting."

A step creaked under Kevin's foot as he shifted his balance. He heard his mother's breath catch.

"Kevin?" she called, raising her voice.

"Yeah," he said, clattering down the stairs to meet them. "You two off?"

"You're sure you don't want to come with us?" his mother asked. "It's a lot warmer out than they predicted for today, you know."

"What? All of forty degrees?" Kevin wrinkled his nose and shuddered. "Be serious. Can you see me at an art fair in the dead of winter, even if the sun *is* trying to come out? You guys'll have fun, but I'd be totally bored *and* frozen. Anyway, I've got plenty of work to keep me busy here." Not homework, he thought, but plenty of exploring work to do. Then he'd let Charley see what an outsider, and an Army brat at that, could do.

"You sure, Kevin?" LTC Spencer managed a shadowed grin. "You could keep me company while your mother buys stuff for us to carry back to the pickup."

Kevin dredged up a laugh to meet his father halfway. "Sorry, Dad," he said. "She's all yours today."

His parents laughed as though everything were normal, and Kevin waved at them as his father put one arm around Kevin's mother and ushered her out the door. He heard the pickup cough a couple of times and finally catch, then he heard it chug down the driveway and out of the housing area.

One thing at a time, he told himself. He'd scope out the house first and try to find the old man's hiding place. Then he'd think about what his father had said. Hadley Proving Ground seemed to be dangerously corrupt, and Kevin just wasn't ready to deal with that yet, or with what his father must be facing every day trying to get his job done.

Instead Kevin went down to the kitchen to get a Pepsi. He knocked on the walls around the pantry, but the space on the far side seemed to be completely filled by the built-in shelves in the dining room where his mother had put their good china and crystal. So far, they hadn't had any dinner guests to get it out for.

Kevin took the can back to his room.

"Hey, Hannibal," he said. "This is the day."

There was a faint rustle inside the hamster's house. Hannibal was a lot more interested in sleeping at this hour than he was in exploring the old Hanson house.

Kevin went into the extra bedroom and checked around the closet there. The space to the side of it seemed filled by his own closet. There was an opening for a crawl space in the bathroom, but when Kevin knocked the panel aside to check it out, he found nothing but pipes and dust. He managed to pull the panel back in place and wipe up the worst of the mess. He took a swig of Pepsi and wondered where to try next.

He examined the little hallway at the top of the stairs that led to the window and apparently nowhere else. He even opened the window and leaned out into the cold. But there were no artificial patches of wall that extended beyond the bricks of the first story. The bathroom on one side seemed to come neatly to the outer wall of the house, and there was nothing, of course, in the empty space over the long, curving staircase itself. Shivering, Kevin slammed the window shut and locked it.

He went back into his own room and slumped to the floor. For a while he sat there, leaning against the wall and drinking Pepsi.

"No luck, Hannibal," he told the hamster, mostly to hear the sound of a voice in the empty house. He wondered where the old man would have done his carving— somewhere quiet, probably, somewhere he wouldn't be interrupted all the time. Definitely somewhere he could make a mess. The crawl space where the original attic might have been still seemed like the best bet, but how could he get up there to check it out? And where could the opening be that old Duane Hanson must have used?

The only other realistic possibility would have been the house's original basement, if it had one. But if that was the hiding place, the carving would be long gone, since the farmhouse had been lifted off its original foundation and moved here to the Post Housing Area. Kevin had to believe the old man's workshop had been moved with the house and was still somewhere he could find.

Kevin suddenly choked on his Pepsi. The slatted attic fan opening over the upstairs hallway for the fan that made such a racket—originally, that could have been an opening for a fold-down set of stairs leading to a real attic! The military had installed the attic fan when they made the house into a set of quarters—why cut a hole if a perfectly good one was already there? All they had to do was tear out the steps and set the fan in the opening. Then Kevin felt his exhilaration ebb away. If that proved Charley's great-grandfather could have gotten up to a workshop in the attic in his own time, it didn't solve the problem of how Kevin was going to get up to it now.

There had to be some way to get into the attic to fix the fan in case it broke, Kevin told himself. It would be dumb to have to get a ladder and climb up on the roof and take out the vent and squeeze in that way every time the fan needed a checkup or an adjustment.

Kevin went back into the hallway and stared up at the attic fan. Where could the entrance be now to whatever crawl space was left around the fan unit? He checked the ceilings in the adjoining bedrooms, but the only openings were heating vents leading down to the basement furnace. He thought about the crawl space he'd found in the bathroom, but that had only opened onto the plumbing, and the tunnel had followed the pipes downstairs to the kitchen and the other bathroom, not up toward the attic.

Kevin glared at the attic fan. There had to be a way to get up there! He looked around. He'd checked the bathroom, his parents' bedroom, their closet, his room, his closet, the extra room and the closet in there, the linen closet—Kevin stopped. He hadn't looked inside the linen closet. He opened the door and looked up. Set into the ceiling, half blocked by two extra pillows his mother had squeezed onto the top shelf, was a push-out crawl-space-access panel.

"Eureka!" Kevin shouted.

He reached up and hauled down the pillows and tossed them onto his parents' bed. He thought about getting a ladder from the garage to climb up but decided it would be easier just to climb the shelves. They were solid two by twelves, and he was sure they'd take his weight. He balanced on the bottom shelf and stretched up until his fingertips touched the access panel. He pushed, and it lifted slightly. Kevin grinned and scrambled up higher until he could get enough leverage to shove the panel up and out completely. Then he climbed into the shadowy attic.

The fan housing took up most of the space now, but Kevin could see the central attic must have once made a comfortable little room. It was insulated, so that in spite of the chill wind creeping in around the fan, Kevin didn't feel too cold. Or maybe it was just the excitement. Kevin felt certain he was finally closing in on the missing carving. He stood in the middle of the attic space and looked around.

The external fan outlet vent took up a large chunk of the ceiling, and Kevin wondered if that might have been a skylight originally. The attic would have made a sunny, cheery workshop for Charley's great-grandfather. He didn't bother looking near the fan housing. If the carving had been hidden there, the workmen would have found it years ago. Anyway, it wasn't likely anybody would hide something special in the center of the attic. There were some old wooden packing crates beside the fan housing, but Kevin was sure the carving wasn't in one of them or it would also have been found.

Where would an adult hide something so a little kid couldn't find it? Kevin figured the two grandsons must have been in and out of the place all the time while their grandfather was working. Maybe the old man had worked on the surprise for the kid early in the morning when the kid was still asleep, or while he was at school. But there would have to be a hiding place he could slip it into the rest of the time.

High up, Kevin decided. If you don't want a short kid to find something, you hide it higher than he can reach, somewhere he can't climb. There must have been a worktable here once, but a kid could climb on top of that to reach something above it. Corners, though, and ceiling beams—maybe the old man had found a place where the wood didn't quite match up with the other walls and had used that for his hiding place. He could slip something in quickly if he heard the kid coming upstairs.

Kevin had just started working his way along the sides of the attic, tapping the upper walls and ceiling, when the phone rang shrilly, startling him. He'd figured with everybody at the Winter Art Fair, this would be one day he wouldn't be interrupted. Brushing off most of the dust, he skidded down the shelves to the floor of the closet and raced into his parents' bedroom to grab the receiver.

≡ 8 ≡

UNEXPECTED COMPANY

"**S**pencer residence," he panted into the receiver.

"Kevin?"

There was a lot of background noise, and Kevin could barely make out his father's voice. He glanced at the clock on his parents' dresser and realized he'd spent a lot more time than he thought. He'd have to hurry if he wanted to explore the attic before his parents came back.

"Yeah, Dad, it's me," he said, catching his breath. "How's the fair?"

"Kevin, I can't hear you too well, but listen to me—we've had some problems down here." Kevin pressed the receiver hard against his ear, trying to make out his father's words through the noise at the far end and the static on the line. "Someone's stolen our pickup."

Kevin stared at the phone in disbelief. "Stolen the pickup?" he shouted. "You're kidding."

"I wish," his father said, his voice fading in and out. "We've reported it to the police, but with the crowd down here and so many out-of-town vehicles they're afraid it's not going to be too easy to find."

"And I'll bet they weren't too helpful to the new Army officer either," Kevin said loudly.

"I don't know," his father told him through the worsening connection. "They were as helpful as they could be, given the circumstances."

An idea started to take shape in the back of Kevin's mind. He shouted into the receiver, "Could this have anything to do with the terrorist threats the Proving Ground was getting, Dad?"

"What? I didn't get all that," his father said. "There's a lot of noise down here. Look, don't worry. It's probably just some kids out for a joyride or something. Once all the confusion from the art fair has calmed down, I'm sure the police will find the truck abandoned on some back road, run out of gas."

Or on a side street somewhere with its tires slashed? Kevin asked himself. He had never said anything about his run-in with Charley's cousin and Duane's threats. Now he realized the month Duane had given him was almost up. It was time his father knew about Duane Hanson.

"Dad, about the pickup," he began, trying to speak clearly and loudly.

"Look, Kevin, don't worry about it," his father said, in the voice he used when he was trying to sound reassuring. "I've got to get off this phone. I just wanted you to know we'll be later than we anticipated getting back home. We're going to have to try to get a taxi, I guess, or wait for the police to drive us, and they're pretty busy with the fair. I just didn't want you to worry about us, okay? We'll get back as soon as we can. 'Bye."

"Dad—"

Kevin pressed the receiver to his ear and listened to the drone of the dial tone through the fuzzy static. If only his father could have heard him better. Should he call the police station? Sure, he told himself. And how much attention would the cops pay to an Army officer's kid at the Proving Ground accusing a local kid of threatening to mess up his father's pickup? Slowly he replaced the receiver and went into his own room.

He lifted the top off Hannibal's cage, opened the house, and reached in to lift out the sleepy hamster. Hannibal protested mildly but relaxed when Kevin held him in his cupped hands up against his chest. Corrupt colonels and cheating test directors and car thieves . . . would the police be any different? And those terrorist threats when they had first come to Hadley—Kevin wondered why he had ever imagined it could be some big international terrorist plot. It had to be local people getting a kick out of making the Proving Ground squirm.

Kevin heard Duane's voice saying, "I'll get you out of Hadley—give it a month. I got it all planned out," as he roared off in his Buick. Were the terrorist threats part of his plan? Each in his own way, Duane and Charley were determined to get even with the Proving Ground because they had the crazy idea it was responsible for destroying their family. Did the theft of the Spencers' pickup figure into Duane's plan?

Kevin's thoughts raced. What was about to happen in Hadley? And was there any way he could prevent it?

Stop it, he told himself angrily. He was wasting time working up a panic over things he couldn't do anything about. He should be concentrating on finding the carving to give Charley. He couldn't locate the stolen truck, or undo the terrorist threats or the cheating at the Proving Ground, but he had to believe he could still change Charley's mind.

He stroked Hannibal's warm fur one more time, then put the hamster back into his cage and secured the lid. Hannibal yawned and stretched, and climbed into his food dish for a snack.

Kevin went back in the hallway and stared up into the linen closet, his fists resting on his hips. He was certain the carving was waiting for him up there. Taking a deep breath, he went in the closet and hauled himself up his makeshift ladder of shelves until he could pull himself back into the attic.

It'll have to be high up, he reminded himself, and went back to exploring the upper wall surfaces and feeling around each beam and support with grim determination. He probed the dusty corners and surprised more than a few drowsy spiders, who scurried away. Then, partway up one corner, his fingers slipped into empty space.

Kevin jerked his hand back instinctively, then cautiously reached through again. He could slip his fingers into the opening easily, but his palm was a tight squeeze. He worked his hand all the way up to the ceiling, then back down. The opening began about five feet above the flooring. Kevin dragged one of the wooden crates over and climbed up to squint at the corner in the dim light. It looked as though some of the boards in the wall on that side of the central attic had never quite met the outer wall of the house. With the overlapping shadows in the attic, the gap was all but invisible.

Kevin reached into the gap again. Near the ceiling he could wedge his hand into the opening up to his wrist, but when he worked down from there, his hand hit something about a foot from the bottom of the open space. Kevin fingered the edges of the object blocking the gap carefully. It *might* be something deliberately wedged into the opening, something slid inside a hiding place. He couldn't reach the back of the thing through the gap, but he tried rocking the top corner to loosen it. It stuck, then with a creak it rocked back slightly and he got the fingers of his other hand underneath it.

Kevin forgot his earlier frustration at problems he couldn't solve. He wiggled the object back and forth with mounting excitement until he had it far enough out of the gap to get a good grip. Then he tugged until it popped out. He climbed down from the wooden crate, wiped his hands on his jeans, and took a good look at what he had found.

It was a flat wooden box. The pale wood was sanded silky smooth under his fingers, even after he brushed away the soft coating of dust. Kevin opened the lid carefully and stared at the contents in surprise. Charley had been wrong. It wasn't a single carving. Her great-grandfather had been making his grandson a set of carvings as a gift. And when Charley saw exactly what the carvings *were*, she was going to be in for a real surprise.

Suddenly Kevin heard a familiar engine getting closer. In the silence around him the stuttering and coughing of their pickup seemed louder than usual. He shut the box and got up quickly. Had his parents gotten the truck back this fast? He'd be in trouble if his mother caught him climbing down through her linen closet covered with fifty years worth of dust.

Peering through the cracks around the fan vent, Kevin saw the pickup chug into their driveway and jerk to a stop, stalling. That wasn't like his father at all. Then the doors opened and two men in Army camouflage uniforms got out. Kevin pulled his head back sharply. Who were they? Had they seen him? He could feel his heart pounding. Security at the Proving Ground didn't wear camouflage uniforms, and there were no regular troops stationed here.

These had to be the guys who had stolen the pickup. Kevin's mouth went dry with the realization. What were the thieves doing here? It was no mystery how they'd gotten past Security at the gate—the idiot on duty had probably just glanced up, seen the uniforms and the Proving Ground sticker on the truck's bumper, and waved them through without paying any attention to the people inside. Kevin remembered his father complaining about the lax security, but nobody had wanted to pay attention to what the new Lieutenant Colonel had to say about anything. He forced himself to swallow, hearing the dry click in his throat. Now that the thieves were in the Proving Ground, was there anything he could do about it?

He heard a splintering sound at the back door and jumped in fear. At the same time he felt a flash of hope. Would anybody else hear it and call Security? Then Kevin remembered the Winter Art Fair with a sinking feeling. There was nobody in the Housing Area to hear—everybody was downtown. With a sudden thrill he realized that the intruders would be expecting him to be downtown too. He could surprise them.

He tried to imagine Orion leaping down from the attic, drawing his sword as he landed in the hallway, confronting the enemy and slashing them to ribbons. The thrill of excitement died away—that image was getting a little faded. It had been so long since he'd played Dungeons & Dragons, Orion hardly seemed real anymore. As long as there were bona fide trolls and demons for Orion to defeat, you could believe he could step into the real world and conquer it, too. But the longer he sat on an index card waiting to enter a new game, the harder he was to imagine.

Kevin strained to listen, feeling as though he'd been frozen in the attic for hours since the two guys had broken in. He had to do something. Where were they now? He thought he heard boots clattering down the basement steps. Was there time for him to climb down and get out of the house? If he could only get outside, he could alert Security himself. Or could he sneak down to his parents' room and phone Security while they were in the basement? But he suspected they'd be sure to hear him if he tried.

He heard a dull clanging far away and wondered what they were doing. There was nothing in the basement except the washer and dryer, and some moving boxes they'd stacked up, and the furnace. What were they banging on? The furnace? Kevin looked at the box he was still holding. That would have to wait. He didn't want to waste time hiding it again, so he just propped it against the wall in one shadowy corner. He wiped his damp hand on his jeans and inched closer to the floor opening.

The boots clattered back up the basement stairs. Kevin gasped and hunched his shoulders unconsciously as he heard glass shatter in the kitchen and then laughter. The laughter sounded strangely familiar. He heard a door slam and then the screech of plastic splintering and a repeated metallic crunch. That was probably his father's stereo.

Kevin clenched his fists. Who were these jerks? What right did they have to come into his house and smash his things? He didn't care if it was Charley herself, for all her justifications of revenge—her great-grandfather would never have condoned this sort of vandalism. This was pure terrorism. Suddenly Kevin remembered Duane's bragging and his earlier suspicion that the terrorist threats might have come from Duane and Pete. Could they be the two thugs wrecking his home now?

If it was Duane and Pete, Kevin wanted to face them, with or without Orion, and make them pay for the damage they were doing. But he stopped at the edge of the opening, realizing it would be suicide to charge these guys like some sort of superhero. He remembered his father's face turning serious after the firebase rescue story, warning him not to sail blindly into battle without having the odds in his favor.

Kevin knew there was a shotgun under his father's side of the bed, but that was useless to him up here. Even if he made it to the bedroom before they ran upstairs and caught him, he wasn't sure he remembered how to pump the slide and get it to fire. The storm troopers downstairs meant business, and the odds would be stacked against him if he just blindly rushed in. After all, the last time he'd seen Duane he'd just kept his cool and not fought back, and he'd been okay. If he sailed into battle today, without any sort of edge, he'd definitely be the one who got totaled. He was sure his father's warning was one hundred percent right.

Leaning over the linen closet, Kevin's nose twitched unpleasantly. He smelled something strange coming up from the house below him, something that overpowered the scents of cedar and mothballs that clung to his mother's blankets. Was the smell from something they'd broken in the kitchen? But it didn't smell like food somehow—it was a thick, heavy smell that made Kevin think of machinery.

He shook his head to clear it as boots stamped across the living room. Whatever the odor was, Kevin didn't have time to worry about it now. He heard metal clang as the floor lamp crashed to the floor, then shattering glass. He groped for the panel and eased it back over the opening. Would they guess he was up here? He had a moment's panic about the pillows, then remembered tossing them onto the bed. They'd look natural enough there. Maybe the guys would just think somebody left the linen closet door open.

He heard the boots stamping up the stairs and wrapped his arms around his knees, suddenly very cold in spite of the attic's insulation. He heard something smash in his parents' room and thought maybe they'd thrown a trinket from the chest of drawers at the mirror. He kept worrying about the pillows and breathed a sigh of relief when the boots tramped down the hall into his room.

"Army brat!" one of them snarled.

Kevin was almost certain he recognized Duane's voice now. This must be the plan he'd been bragging about to Pete. But why trash the house? It was the Hansons' house too. He heard wood splintering and thought it must be his chair. There wasn't much in his room to break.

Then he heard a scrape of plastic and another crash.

Suddenly he heard a loud squeaking drowned out by cruel laughter.

The crash—Kevin realized they must have thrown down the hamster cage. He felt a sickening jolt of fear flare up in his chest. Hannibal would only squeak if he were terrified—or was he hurt?

The fear turned into rage. Kevin forgot his father's warning. He forgot his father had said he could have been killed or court martialed if he had failed in the rescue attempt. He forgot Orion wasn't real. He grabbed the panel blocking the access and flung it aside. He didn't care that he wasn't an Army officer or a Dungeons & Dragons hero.

Kevin clutched the lip of the opening and swung himself out of the attic and onto the floor of the linen closet. Then he raced for his room.

≡9≡

THE TERRORISTS

Duane was standing in the doorway. He had his black combat boots planted wide and the legs of his uniform were neatly tucked into the tops and bloused out, just the way Kevin's father wore his. Beyond him, Kevin got a quick glimpse of the cage lying under the window, sharp splinters of plastic scattered on the carpet. The house had tipped over and Kevin could see inside. There was no sign of Hannibal.

Duane was just turning to see what the unexpected noise was when Kevin lowered his head and tackled him. The two boys crashed to the floor, the air exploding out of Duane in a startled *Oof!* Kevin freed himself and saw Pete coming toward him. He had just enough time to think how un-soldierlike Pete looked slouching in a wrinkled version of the same uniform Duane was wearing before he cannonballed into the other boy's legs and tripped him. Then, leaving the two of them tangled on the floor gasping for breath, Kevin looked frantically around for the terrified hamster.

He quickly checked Hannibal's usual hiding places under the bed, scanned behind books in the bottom shelf, glanced in the corners—could Hannibal have squeezed under the closet door if he were terrified enough?

Kevin grabbed at his wastebasket, lying on its side, and pulled out handfuls of crumpled paper in case the hamster had tried to nest in it. But there was no sign of him. Kevin heard wood splinter as a boot went for something just behind him, but he dodged away. He saw a flash of movement behind a desk leg and reached quickly for Hannibal. Just as he had the hamster cupped firmly in his hands, Kevin felt a fist grab his shirt collar and jerk him to his feet. Duane twisted him around and glared.

"You're going to be real sorry you did that, Army brat."

Kevin slipped the trembling hamster into his shirt pocket. There were some food pellets left over from the last time Hannibal had been there, and the frightened animal curled up quickly. Kevin clenched his fists and tried to glare back.

"You're going to be sorry yourself," he snapped. "Breaking into people's houses, smashing up their stuff. You're into major criminal charges here."

Duane snorted. Behind him, Pete managed a faint chuckle. He was standing just outside the door, slapping a thick blackjack awkwardly into one gloved hand, and Kevin had the sudden impression that Pete would rather be someplace else. Could he use that somehow?

Feeling bolder, Kevin demanded, "What did you

think you were doing anyway, tormenting a defenseless animal? Picking on people is one thing, but—"

Kevin couldn't remember what he had planned to say. He did remember he had intended to follow his father's warning and stay hidden. He felt his mouth go dry as Duane lifted his right hand and the light ran down the glittering blade of his knife, but he remembered Hannibal's squeak and held his ground.

"Are you finished, Army brat?" Duane asked, flexing his hand so the steel blade flashed.

"Oh, he's finished all right," Pete said. "He is history."

"What are you doing here?" Kevin asked. He was afraid it would come out a dry croak, but his voice sounded strong, nowhere near as shaky as he felt inside.

"It's my house, remember?" Duane told him.

"Not anymore," Kevin said.

Duane's face contorted and he started to answer something, but Pete nudged him from behind. "Come on, man, let's quit wasting time." Pete's eyes were darting back and forth as though he expected somebody to walk in on them any minute.

Duane grinned. It was the same slow, cold smile Kevin remembered so clearly from the parking lot. "Don't sweat it," he said. "We've got time."

Pete fumbled with his gloved hand to jerk up the loose camouflage sleeve over his watch. "It's after two already—people'll be coming back from the Art Fair soon, and Security's going to make a pass sooner or later."

Duane shook his head. "My father said the Proving Ground Security is on half staff until six tonight. The guys on duty won't be bothering about the Housing Area or the test ranges this afternoon."

Pete jerked his thumb at Kevin. "What about his parents? They'll be back as soon as they can hook a ride."

"No time soon," Duane told him. "That's all part of the plan, remember? Jim Dickson's got the desk and dispatch this afternoon at the city police station, and he hates the Army like poison—his cousin got fired from the Proving Ground for working short hours during harvest. He won't be in any rush to get a car to drive the Spencers back home."

"I still don't think we ought to be wasting time," Pete said. He licked his lips nervously. Kevin thought he looked like a mad scientist who'd created a monster, and the monster had gotten away from him. It was one thing to egg Duane on the way Pete had done in the school parking lot. It was another to see Duane taking charge.

"Well, what do we do about the kid?" Pete demanded.

Duane shrugged. "For now, we take him with us. I don't want him grabbing the phone and warning the main gate the minute we drive out of here. Once we're finished, I can decide what to do with him."

Kevin found his voice. "I'm not going anywhere with you."

Duane laughed again. "You'll do what we tell you, Army brat—you got that? Or do you want me to let Pete give that little rat of yours a couple of love taps with his blackjack?" He shook his head. "What a baby pet for a big, brave Army boy to have!"

Kevin didn't bother to take the bait. Instead, he buttoned the flap of his shirt pocket over Hannibal. "It takes some big, bold macho jerk to threaten to kill a little animal," he said. "In my book that makes you real chicken meat."

Duane lunged forward, but Pete grabbed his arm and jerked him back. "Stop and think about this, okay? We can't take the kid with us! And we can't just leave him anyplace—he's seen us, he knows. He'll blow the whole thing!"

"Not before it's done," Duane said. "Who's going to believe him, anyway?"

"Try his father," Pete said. "Try the Army. They'll listen to him, even if they aren't sure he's telling the truth. And once word gets out, you're sunk."

Kevin wanted to promise them he wouldn't tell, but he couldn't get the words out. He was determined to call Security and the police as soon as he could get to a phone, and he couldn't seem to lie about it.

"You don't just make things up as you go along, you know," Duane was telling Pete. "You plan. And before I change the plan, I have to think it through."

"There's no time to think," Pete snapped, trying to get back in control. "All you ever do is talk about your great master plan—you wouldn't even be doing this today if I hadn't pushed you into it. Now you just want to go back to making your plans—this time you gotta *do* something, and fast!"

"You don't plan, you make mistakes," Duane said. "You make mistakes, you get caught. We can't jeopardize the mission."

Pete groaned. "You let this creep blab about us and you definitely jeopardize your lousy mission."

"So shut up and let me think," Duane said.

Kevin waited in the sudden silence, not meeting Pete's glare or Duane's frown. His nose twitched and he realized that the heavy, sickening smell seemed to be getting worse.

"What is that?" he demanded. "What did you break open that smells so bad?"

Duane laughed. "You like that smell, kid? We're thinking of calling it eau de arson."

"What?" Kevin felt a burning fear slowly uncoil in his stomach.

"Fuel oil," Duane told him. "It's a little sweet, but after it's had a chance to breathe for a while, I think it'll come into its own. And once we finish the mission— poof! Torched house."

Pete grinned suddenly, as if he'd finally thought of something good about the situation. "You want us to leave you and your little rat here for the party? Crispy, crunchy, Government-issue toasted dependents?"

"You're crazy!" Kevin shouted, his fists clenched. His mind tried to find its way through the confusion. What had they done before they broke into his house? What was Duane's mission? And how could he break away from them and alert Security?

"Shut up!" Duane shouted back. He glared at Kevin. "Who the hell are you calling crazy, Army brat? We're not the ones who came in here and threw people out of their homes. We're not the ones who murdered old men. We're not the ones who blow things up all the time. *You're* the crazy ones, Army scumbag—and now you're going to pay!"

Duane looked at Pete. "I've decided—we take him with us. It'll make the odds on getting out higher, and as long as he's with us he can't stop the plan."

Kevin felt Hannibal move in his pocket and his mind raced as he tried to decide what to do about the hamster. He flicked through the options in his mind—each one was worse than the last. He discarded one after another until he ran out. If Duane's plan worked, whatever it was, this house was going to turn into a fireball before the afternoon was over. And even if the place didn't burn, the fumes from the fuel oil wouldn't be good for Hannibal. The smell was already making Kevin feel sick. What would it do to the hamster if Kevin left him exposed to it all afternoon?

Where could he leave him, anyway? The cage was smashed. Kevin could leave him in the bathtub, maybe, with some things from his cage, and hope he didn't escape before the Spencers came home, but Hannibal was good at escaping. And the hamster had been badly frightened—if he was left alone in a strange place, he was sure to try to get out.

There were no good choices. Kevin realized he'd have

to take the hamster with him. He felt a hysterical urge to laugh, standing there amid the wreckage of his room, about to set out on the run with two insane teenage arsonists and one hamster in contravention of every order his father had ever given him—what in the world was LTC Spencer going to say when he came home?

And would he have a home to come back to, or only the charred remains?

"Get moving, Army brat," Duane said. Pete was already clattering down the stairs.

Kevin reached for a sweatshirt lying where one of the boys had thrown it. He pulled it over the lump Hannibal made in his pocket and followed Pete. Behind him Duane punched him in the small of his back.

"Move out smartly, punk," he ordered.

Kevin tried not to look at the wreck they'd made of the living room. He pulled his coat out of the mess they'd left in the open hall closet and slowly drew it on. "Where are you taking me?"

Duane shoved him toward the front door. "You'll find out soon enough."

Kevin started to zip his coat, and Duane swore. "Just get moving, punk. Don't worry, it isn't cold out there; you won't freeze." He laughed, and in front of them Pete chuckled a little.

"If anything," Pete said, "he'll melt."

Behind him, Kevin heard Duane smash the glass in the front door. Then Pete grabbed his sleeve and hurried him to the pickup. Kevin got a quick glimpse of a red gas can and some sort of bundle in the bed of the truck and, incongruously, a blue-and-white plastic cooler. The dark cloth around the bundle lifted and rippled in the wind.

Duane cranked the starter and stomped on the gas, and the pickup roared to life. "This is one lousy truck," he told Kevin.

Pete shoved Kevin into the cab beside Duane, then climbed in and reached for the door handle.

Before the latch caught, Duane was backing out of the driveway. Kevin slumped down in the seat, barely paying attention to the direction the jouncing truck was taking. There was only one gate, after all, when they were ready to leave. Or were they planning more destruction inside the Proving Ground? Kevin concentrated on trying to come up with some way to escape from the two boys.

He jumped in surprise when the pickup jolted to a stop and stalled.

"Move," Duane ordered, and Kevin slid out of the truck beside Pete. He looked around, blinking in the hazy winter sunlight, thinking about making a run for it. This part of the Proving Ground didn't look familiar. There were fragments of metal in the dirt, and concrete barricades set up at intervals. But there was nowhere for Kevin to run, nowhere he could hide from them. The place was completely deserted except for a deer grazing just north of them, upwind. It ignored them completely.

"Point Tango," Duane said with satisfaction. "Demolitions."

As Kevin watched, Duane lifted the cooler out of the pickup and motioned to Pete to get the bundle. Duane took some gloves out of his belt, pulled them on, and lifted the lid off the cooler. He reached inside and took out a block of ice.

Kevin looked closer. It wasn't just ice—it looked like an oversized ice cube with a big green egg growing out of the top. The egg looked very familiar to him, and he wondered if he had finally flipped out. There was a ring attached to the top of the egg, and Kevin was sure he'd seen those things before in snapshots from Vietnam of his father in web gear.

"What is that?" he asked, disbelieving.

"He hasn't been introduced," Duane said, gesturing with the block of ice. "Punk, meet Willie Peter. Willie Peter, meet the Army brat."

"Willie Peter?" Kevin wondered if he'd stepped into the Twilight Zone. What kind of idiot joked about something this dangerous?

Duane settled the block of ice carefully on a flat patch of ground. "Willie Peter," he said cheerfully. "White phosphorus."

Kevin felt the energy run out of his arms and legs like water. He sagged back against the pickup, feeling the wind suddenly ice cold on his face. He had known all along that was what it was. "That's a grenade," he whispered.

"Give the Army brat a gold star," Duane announced.

Pete laughed a little as he dropped the bundle on the ground next to Duane and went back to the truck.

"What are you trying to do?" Kevin asked. He couldn't believe what he was seeing, and his words stumbled out weak and disconnected. He wasn't even certain he'd spoken them aloud.

But Duane heard him. He turned around and fixed his eyes on Kevin. "The Proving Ground is going to have a little accident this afternoon, Army brat, and I'm trying to help it happen."

He nodded at the metal-studded earth around them. "Demolitions," he said. "My father works here. They blow things up. Sometimes they try to blow things up and they don't blow. Sometimes the duds blow later. This baby's going to blow later today."

Kevin shook his head. "But what's the point?"

Duane flipped open the bundle and some of the straw inside fell out.

"White phosphorus burns on contact with air," he told Kevin. "For an Army brat you don't know much, do you? They even teach you that in junior high chemistry. So the grenade bursts, the white phosphorus splatters out everywhere, like a lawn sprinkler shooting fire. The white phosphorus flares like a match the minute it hits the open air, and it sticks to whatever it hits. Whatever it sticks to starts to burn too."

"You're going to start a fire?" Kevin asked stupidly.

"Straw, sprinkled with a little diesel to ensure a good

blaze, and poof—torch time." Pete dropped the red gas can on the dirt near the bundle of straw.

"And we'll be far away," Duane said, "ready to join the rest of Hadley in condemning the Proving Ground for being a hazard to the farms and the town."

"It's a grenade," Kevin said slowly, trying to follow their thinking. "You pull the pin and throw the grenade. That lever on the side, the bail, it flies up without the pin and the grenade goes off and the white phosphorus shoots out, right? How are you going to be far away when the fire starts?"

Duane laughed. "That's all part of the plan, punk—that's what the ice is for." He pointed at the phosphorus grenade embedded in the block of ice. "The ice is holding the bail down. After I pull the pin, the bail can't come up until the ice melts. It's warmer today than I expected, but it'll still take a while, and we'll be long gone."

He stood up and reached his arms above his head, his fingers outstretched. He grinned at Kevin. "It'll be like a million kitchen match heads all flaring up at once here—phosphorus everywhere, torching the straw, then the grass. The phosphorus will keep burning for a long time, even after it sticks. Everything's been so dry for so long it should burn even without the diesel, but it pays to be sure."

He lowered his hands and glanced at the Housing Area. "Nobody's going to realize what's happening right away, especially with so many people down at that Art

Fair. With Security short staffed for the fair, the fire'll be out of control before they know it and heading right for the Housing Area."

Duane looked back at Kevin, his eyes hard. "Oh, I don't figure all the houses will burn, but I made sure no Army scum would ever live in the Hanson house again. That was part of the plan."

The fuel oil, Kevin realized. They must have burst open the furnace in the basement and soaked the place with fuel oil. When the fire reached the house, it'd go off like a firecracker.

Then he thought of the carvings he'd found. Duane was going to destroy his great-grandfather's carvings. Kevin started to say something, then swallowed the words. He didn't think Duane would care about saving anything if that got in the way of his revenge.

The wind scattered some of the straw Pete was spreading, and Kevin realized there was a much bigger danger than the loss of the carvings.

"Do you realize which way the wind is blowing?" he asked.

"Yeah," Duane told him, "right toward the Housing Area."

"And right toward the town after that," Kevin said.

"That's the idea," Pete said. Now that they were out of the house and doing something, his nervousness seemed to have lessened. He actually seemed to be enjoying himself.

Duane nodded. "This is the only way to show everybody how dangerous the Proving Ground is—to make them feel the heat a little." He shrugged. "They'll put it out before it reaches town, but everybody's going to start screaming what if—and they'll close this place at last." Duane smiled in satisfaction.

Kevin stared at him. Duane had to be completely insane. Hadley was a forest fire waiting to happen; he'd realized that from the first moment he'd seen the "controlled burning" of the undergrowth. Between the drought-stricken land and this steady wind, once the fire took hold, they'd never put it out. It wasn't only the Housing Area that would burn—all the offices and maintenance buildings would go. The trees and the dry undergrowth would catch, and then the fire would just race through the woods to the farms and out into the fields. The dry cornstalks would turn into a giant sheet of flame.

Pete laughed. "Don't look so shocked, kid. Duane here's been saying he'd get even with this place for killing his great-grandfather, and now he's finally doing it."

Duane nodded. "Now everybody's going to know at last just how dangerous the Proving Ground is."

You're the one who's dangerous, Kevin thought, but he kept it to himself. "What if they can't put it out?" he demanded. "What if the fire spreads through the farms and into town?"

"It won't," Duane said flatly. "And if it singes the edges a little, it'll just be more of a scare, won't it?"

"But the wind gusts," Kevin said desperately. "Everything's so dry the wind's going to send your explosion out of control."

"Just shut up, Army brat," Duane snapped. "I've got the plan all worked out. Dangerous explosion, fire inside the Proving Ground, big scare, end of Proving Ground. And that's it."

"Straw's spread," Pete announced. He hefted the gas can. "Shall I start pouring?"

Duane nodded. "Keep most of it downwind of the grenade," he said. He stood up and shoved Kevin toward the cooler. "Make yourself useful, punk," he ordered. "Shut the cooler and put it back in the bed of the truck."

Numbly, Kevin reached over and pushed the lid back down. He lifted the empty cooler up over the side of the truck and let it drop with a dull thud onto the metal bed. On the other side of the truck, Pete saluted and started splashing diesel on the ground. He whistled in time to the splashes.

Duane knelt beside the block of sweating ice. "Now I pull the pin," he said.

Pete's whistling cut off abruptly, and Duane laughed again. "Don't worry—remember the plan. This is totally safe."

Kevin held his breath. If that thing went off, they were all done for, regardless of Duane's plan.

Duane glanced back. "Finish up with that and put the can in the truck bed," he told Pete.

He casually tossed some of the straw close to the block of ice so the phosphorus would be sure to land on it. He picked up a few rocks and scattered them over the straw to anchor it in place. Then he crouched there, dusting his hands, and smiling at the frozen grenade.

"All set," Pete called. Kevin noticed he had half-hidden himself behind the cab of the pickup.

"Then I guess it's zero hour," Duane said. He reached out and gripped the slippery block of ice in one hand, then jerked the pin out of the grenade.

≡ **10** ≡
ESCAPE

Kevin watched the Security Guard gatehouse grow larger in the windshield. Duane drove carefully, keeping under the Proving Ground speed limit. He was riding the clutch because the pickup kept shuddering, protesting that the speed was somewhere between its third and fourth gears. Kevin couldn't get the irrelevant thought out of his mind that his father would be really angry if Duane messed up the clutch.

Nothing had happened when Duane pulled the pin on the white-phosphorus grenade. The grenade just sat there, the thick block of ice holding the bail in place. Duane had crouched beside it, grinning up at them, swinging the pin on its ring around one finger.

"Time to move out smartly," he ordered, and he'd stood up and given Kevin a shove toward the pickup. Kevin climbed in, squashed between Pete and Duane, and turned back for a last look at the frozen grenade. The ice had turned cloudy in the air. That frost was the first step in thawing.

"How long will it take?" he asked.

"Wouldn't you like to know?" Pete snapped.

"Long enough," Duane told him.

How long was long enough? Kevin wondered. Long enough for Duane and Pete to be well away, fixing their alibi. How much time did that give him to get back to the grenade and prevent it from going off?

The thought shocked him. He, Kevin Spencer, wasn't going anywhere near that grenade again. He'd alert Security, or the Fire Department, or somebody else who knew what they were doing, and they'd take care of it. Anybody but him.

The wind whistled through the loose pickup doors as they drove toward the exit. "Hey," Kevin said desperately, "can't you hear that wind? Don't you know what it's going to do to your fire once it starts?"

"Shut up, Army brat," Duane snapped. "I told you— the plan is for the fire to threaten the town. The wind is just going to make the point better, that's all."

Pete rapped Kevin's knee with the blackjack, hard, and Kevin choked back a cry. "Shut up, creep." He looked angrily at Duane. "You should have listened to me—I'm supposed to be calling the shots! I said not to bring the kid—he's a troublemaker."

"Put a lid on it," Duane said sharply. He was coming up on the Security checkpoint and his attention was focused on the door the guard would come out through.

Kevin rubbed his knee and looked anxiously for the guard. Come on, he concentrated, willing whoever was on duty to receive his thoughts. For once, really look at us. Don't just glance at the truck, *see* who's driving it—shut the gates, stop the truck—do something!

"Don't even think it, scumbag."

Duane's voice was hard and cold. He capped the warning by deftly sliding his switchblade out of his pocket and flipping it across Kevin to Pete. Pete frowned unhappily at the knife, but he carefully flicked the blade out and pressed it against Kevin's side.

Kevin knew it had to be his imagination, but he was sure he could feel the point through his insulated ski jacket, through the thick sweatshirt and the flannel shirt and the cotton T-shirt underneath, pressing cold and needle sharp just above his kidney.

"I'm not going anywhere," he said. That pricking in his side *had* to be imagination.

"Just don't get any smart ideas about warning the Security Guard," Duane said. He jammed the clutch in all the way and downshifted, slowing outside the gatehouse. He glanced out the windshield at the gate. "A few more yards and we're home free, but if you make trouble, you and that little rat of yours pay the price."

Kevin didn't bother to answer. He just kept thinking with all his might at the guard—look, just *look* at us. . . .

The pickup rolled to a stop. Duane kept the clutch in and shifted into first gear, ready to pop the clutch and make his escape. Pete slumped slightly back in his seat, partially shielding himself from the guard's view behind Kevin. Out of the corner of his eye Kevin saw the guard stand up and start slowly toward the door. Then the phone rang loudly in the guardhouse. Duane jumped slightly at the unexpected sound.

Don't answer it, Kevin willed the guard. Look at us— the phone can't be as important as this—

But the guard shot a quick glance at the military sticker on the bumper without even opening the guardhouse door and stepping out to see who was inside the truck. He waved them through while he was turning back to pick up the receiver. Duane eased up on the clutch and drove decorously through the gate. Once he hit the main road, he gunned the motor and shifted quickly to get up to speed.

"All right!" he yelled. "We did it!"

Pete closed the switchblade and tossed it to Duane. "Mission accomplished, General?" he asked, sneering a little, but sounding strangely pleased, too.

Duane caught the knife one handed and slid it back into his pocket. "Mission accomplished—once we get rid of the truck."

"And what about the punk?" Pete asked, his pleasure disappearing. He elbowed Kevin. "How do we get rid of him? You gotta face it, pal—he can make trouble for us."

Surprisingly, Duane laughed. He shot Kevin a sly smile. "Too late now, Army brat—that baby's gonna blow. And whether you like it or not, you're gonna be just as responsible as we are."

Kevin's outraged, "What do you mean?" overlapped Pete's exclamation.

Duane's grin widened. "The plan—I made the plan fit the problem. Remember that cooler, punk? Well, now it's got your fingerprints all over it. And that security guard saw you in the truck with us. You try to finger us and they investigate—the evidence will tell them you were part of the team. And how's your precious Army going to like that?"

"They'll never believe it," Kevin sputtered. "My dad—he'd never buy it! Nobody else on post would either!" But he felt a surge of doubt, remembering Chris Waverly. He'd be all too ready to testify that Kevin had turned his back on the Army and joined up with the Hadley kids.

Pete was considering the idea, frowning. "I don't know, man. The kid could be right about his father. The Army would believe an officer, wouldn't they? And wouldn't the Colonel who runs the Proving Ground believe him too?"

"You don't know what you're talking about!" Duane snapped. He turned off the main road at the southern edge of the Proving Ground and the truck bounced down a deserted rural road. "You want to know what the Colonel's going to say? Spencers are troublemakers, that's what he'll say."

Kevin got a sudden sick feeling, remembering his father's complaints about the Colonel turning a blind eye to the falsified test results.

"Pop says LTC Spencer's done nothing but make trouble since he came to the Proving Ground. If the evidence proves the little punk was in on it, no matter what his father says, the Colonel will believe the evidence."

"But even if the evidence points toward him—" Pete's

face was flushed now, and his fists were kneading the blackjack nervously against his knees.

Duane slapped the steering wheel impatiently. "Shut up, Pete! Nobody's going to find out anything unless the stupid punk blabs. The point, punk"—he punched Kevin's arm for emphasis—"is that you'll keep quiet if you know what's good for you. If you drop the ax on us, it cuts off your head too—so how do you like that?"

Pete was shaking his head in short, sharp jerks. "I don't like it, Duane. We should never have taken him with us—I said we should leave him in the house—you should have listened to me!" His voice began to rise sharply.

"Shut up!" Duane screamed. He rubbed the side of his head. "*You* don't like it—so who cares what you think? You didn't think I'd ever go through with my mission, but I did. I don't have to listen to you—*I'm* the one in charge here, *I'm* the one who makes the plan!"

"Your plan isn't going to work!" Pete snapped back. "Quit playing soldier games and get real!"

"All right!" Duane said sharply, his eyes going cold. "You want a real solution? We kill him."

Kevin thought all the air inside the cab must have vanished without warning. His lungs locked and the world reeled around him. Pete seemed strangely quiet beside him.

"Stage an accident with the truck," Duane was saying from a long way away, "make sure the kid dies in it—all loose ends tied up. If they find the cooler with his prints in the back when they find the body, they'll figure he planned the whole thing with some friends. We're out of it."

Pete's mouth was working, but no sounds came out. "Kill him?" he finally croaked.

Kevin discovered he'd started breathing again. He had to think what to do—Duane wanted him to go along with his crazy mission. Kevin could either obey Duane and keep his mouth shut, or he could let Duane kill him.

And he had no doubt that Duane would kill him in a heartbeat.

"Don't act crazy," Pete stammered. "I never said we'd kill anybody! You can't do that!"

Duane laughed, and the sound was as chilling as the frozen grenade back at the Proving Ground. "I can do anything I need to if it'll accomplish the mission. I can kill him as easily as I'd step on an ant. And you'll do it with me."

Doesn't he know I'm listening? Kevin thought wildly. Does he think I'd just let him kill me—the way I let him trash the house while I hid in the attic? Then his stomach heaved, and he realized if he didn't stop Duane this time, he wouldn't have any life left to go through, hiding in attics or not. If he was ever serious about standing up for himself, if he expected to survive this afternoon, now was the time to take action.

"You think you can push people into doing things, Pete, and then play it safe," Duane was saying. He slammed his fist down on the steering wheel. "Well, it doesn't work that way! You're part of my mission now, pal. It's Plan *A* or Plan *B*. Either we keep him quiet or we kill him."

"Forget about your stupid plans!" Pete's voice rose to a hysterical shriek. "I'm not getting involved in killing anybody, and I'm not going to jail because *you* wanted to get even with the Proving Ground! I say we cut our losses right now—pack up and get out of Hadley for good!"

"You're going to do what I say we have to do!" Duane shouted. "I'm in charge!"

Kevin's mind raced. Escape—how could he do it, short of shoving Pete out of the speeding pickup and jumping, hoping he didn't break a leg or turn an ankle? Orion would have flattened Pete and been out the door already, but Kevin knew he wasn't the Dungeons & Dragons ranger. Anyway, what would happen to Hannibal if he jumped? He'd always suspected Hannibal would sleep through a roller-coaster ride if he was settled in his warm pocket, but this would be the acid test.

The first step had to be getting out of the truck. And for the escape to succeed, Kevin had to make everything possible work in his favor. He glanced out the window. They were south of the Proving Ground, driving past a series of small farms. He saw some cows with shaggy coats in one field and rows of dry, barren cornstalks in another. The sight of the corn gave him a new surge of anger. Once the fire jumped the fence around the Proving Ground, it would race through the withered corn.

Ahead on the right, Kevin saw a farmhouse that looked even more beat up than the others. The lower framework was neatly built of gray stones, but the wooden boards above the stonework showed plainly through the weathered and peeling paint. A pole barn near the farmhouse was half hidden by a sagging shed built of gray, weathered boards. The shed door flapped stiffly in the wind. And Kevin thought he saw a black space in the barn's gray board wall—either another open door or a window.

There was a stop sign on the corner, and Kevin suddenly made up his mind. He went limp and let his body slump against Duane, then caught his breath as though waking up and tried to straighten. He reached out and grabbed the wheel to pull himself upright, jerking the truck sharply to the right and into the stop sign with a scream of metal as the truck stalled.

"Stupid Army brat!" Duane snapped, shoving Kevin away from him.

"I—I'm sorry," Kevin stammered, making himself sound weak and frightened. "I didn't mean—I just—"

"Little punk fainted! And now the lousy truck's busted!" Pete shoved his door open, jumped out, and stumbled frantically to check the damage.

"Get back inside!" Duane shouted, and slammed the gearshift into neutral. Kevin kept still while Duane ground the key in the starter and the engine stalled again.

Now! Kevin told himself.

He shot across the seat and dropped out of the cab, his right hand cupped outside Hannibal's pocket, holding the hamster secure. He hit the drainage ditch rolling, then picked himself up at the bottom and was up the other side and running across the field toward the shed. His knee throbbed where Pete had hit it, but he ignored the pain.

Behind him Duane cursed furiously.

"Up that way!" Pete shouted. "What do we do now?"

"The engine's flooded—go after him!"

The voices got fainter as Kevin raced toward the shed.

"I don't know this place . . . come with me . . ."

". . . can't leave it in the middle of the intersection . . ."

The wind eased up suddenly and the shed door swung shut in front of Kevin, then a new gust blew it open again. Kevin ducked inside, grabbed the metal handle, and slammed the door shut. He fumbled for the latch in the dimness and hooked the door securely closed. That gave him a chance to catch his breath, but he knew the latch wouldn't hold Duane or Pete for long. He could feel the hamster rustling around in his pocket, but Hannibal seemed more irritated than frightened. He was already settling down again.

Kevin scanned the shed as his eyes got used to the darkness. There was a rickety workbench on the far side with a clutter of odd tools and rusty tin cans filled with nails and screws and nuts and bolts. The wind whistled through an empty window frame over the table. Shreds of opaque plastic hung from the wooden frame, and through the opening Kevin could see the barn. He'd been right—the top half of one of the doors was hanging open! If he could squeeze through the window and make it to the barn before the others realized what he'd done, perhaps he could find a good hiding place and outwait them.

Kevin climbed up onto the workbench, feeling the legs creak and sway unsteadily under him. He stuck his head through the window for a quick glance around. The back of the shed was shielded from the road by the house, so he might be able to reach the barn without either Pete or Duane seeing him.

Behind him, he heard boots thudding across the field toward the door.

"Come on, punk, open up—we know you're in there." Pete's voice was low and terrified and sounded like he was repeating words he'd heard on some cop show on TV. Kevin caught a muffled pounding on the wood. Why was Pete being so quiet? He'd expected a full-power assault on the shed the moment anyone reached it.

The pickup coughed from the intersection, then revved into action. Duane must have coaxed the flooded engine back to life. Kevin pulled his head back inside and shoved one leg through the window. He twisted on the workbench as quietly as possible and kicked out the other foot. Once he got his hips through, he could turn on his stomach and brace his feet against the outside wall and ease his upper body through without squashing Hannibal against the window frame. He had to twist his shoulders to get the right angle to force them through, but then he popped out and slid gently to the ground. He dashed for the barn, refusing to let his sore knee slow him down, and pulled himself up and over the half-door, dropping down inside, hidden from view.

Outside, Kevin heard the pickup stall again, then the banging of a door. Had either of them seen him run for the barn? If not, they'd waste time trying to break open the latched door, thinking he'd still be inside.

"Give me that," Duane said, more loudly. "We'll have to break the latch."

"Keep it down," Pete snapped, softer. "What if somebody's home?"

"They'll be at the Art Fair," Duane said.

"What if they're not? If anybody sees us, we're dead."

"When I catch him, he's dead," Duane promised.

Kevin got to his feet slowly. Their arguing was going to save him after all. All he had to do was find a secure place to hide. The longer Duane had to look to find him, the more upset Pete would be about someone catching them. And Pete was pretty uptight about things already.

He knew they couldn't see him from the front of the shed. Carefully he reached out and caught the open half door and pulled it to him. Both the upper and lower doors had bolts on the inside, and he threw the top one, locking it securely. Now the only light around him was what filtered through the cracks in the warped boards.

Kevin picked his way slowly through the crowded barn, careful not to bump into anything or make any noise that might give him away. How long would it take them to break open the latch? It was a simple hook, but Duane wouldn't be able to see that from the outside. Kevin edged around a tractor and stopped suddenly to let a shadowy clutter of mowing and plowing attachments take shape before he crashed into them. He carefully climbed over one end of a tiller and eased his way farther into the darkness.

A loose pile of burlap sacking was lying in one corner, behind the combine. Part of the pile seemed to be draped over some tools. Kevin thought he saw a shovel and a mattock protruding from a ragged edge of burlap. If he could cover himself with some of the other sacking, perhaps they wouldn't notice him even if they found another way into the barn.

Trying not to disturb the tools, Kevin squatted down on the dusty floor and eased himself under the sacking. The burlap smelled dry and musty and he almost sneezed, but he took a deep breath and pinched his nose and ordered himself not to. The sneeze finally disappeared, and Kevin scrunched down, making himself as small under the sacking as he could. He propped up a pick beside him and draped the burlap over that, making a little tent for himself. If they didn't look too closely—if they were nervous enough and hurried enough, he might just make it.

Kevin heard the shed door bang open. Now Duane

and Pete were inside. He heard a faint curse, then an unintelligible murmur of voices. Any minute now they'd figure out he'd escaped through the window. They'd look and they'd see the barn—but would they remember the door had been open before?

He heard the shed door bang again and their boots pounding across the ground. It was still hard to hear their voices.

". . . he's gone now . . . get out of here." That might have been Pete's voice.

". . . around here somewhere . . ." That had to be Duane. ". . . a minute . . . wasn't . . . door open?"

Kevin caught his breath and pressed himself tightly against the floor. Any second now Duane was going to insist they look inside the barn.

≡ 11 ≡

RACE AGAINST TIME

"**. . . C**razy . . . door locked . . ." Pete's
faint voice sounded frightened and impatient. ". . . long
gone . . ."

Duane's voice suddenly sounded so clear that Kevin
jumped. He must be standing just on the other side of
the wall where Kevin lay hidden. "Yeah, the door's
locked now, but I'm sure it was open when the punk lit
out of the truck."

"So what?" Kevin strained to hear Pete's voice more
clearly. "He probably locked it to confuse us like he did
with the shed. Come on, we've got to get out of here
before anyone sees us."

"You're just glad he's disappeared." Duane's voice was
contemptuous. "You didn't want to take the responsibility of killing him—I bet you're hoping we never find
him."

"Forget about him," Pete begged, still keeping his
voice low. "We've got to cover our asses now, man."

"First we find the Army brat and take care of him."
Duane's voice was fainter. Kevin heard something bang a
couple of times, then a clang of metal and a wooden thud.

"Come on," Duane called, his voice loud now. "Side door. He's got to be inside somewhere."

Kevin hunched down as low as he could get and tried to breathe in slow, steady, silent breaths. He heard boots crossing the hard-packed earth.

"I'll look on this side," Duane said. "You check out those bales of hay."

"Screw the hay—I just want out of here," Pete said nervously, but Kevin heard a second pair of boots stamping dully across the barn floor.

Then he heard a muffled crash, a surprised shout from Duane, and a string of curses from Pete.

"What the hell are you doing?" Duane's voice came from just in front of the combine. Kevin held his breath, then the boots strode away from him.

"My leg," Pete gasped shrilly. "Tore it—"

Duane swore. "That was a bale of barbed wire for fencing, you idiot. Can't you do anything?"

"I can get out of here!" Pete screamed, his nerve finally snapped. "I can drive the truck too, you know, and I've had it with your crazy mission! You can come with me or spend the rest of your life playing hide-and-seek in this barn, for all I care. Nobody's here—do you hear me? Nobody's here!"

Kevin heard Pete limp toward the side door, and Duane followed him.

"Just let me check out the rest of the barn," Duane said. "Wait in the truck, okay?"

"Forget the little punk!" Pete cried. "Let him squeal.

I'm getting out of Hadley while I still can, and if you've got any brains, you'll be right behind me!"

A few moments later Kevin heard the truck starter churn sluggishly. Then the engine coughed and roared to life.

"Pete!"

Kevin strained to hear over the stuttering engine. Were those boots he heard running? Duane's boots? Or was it his imagination? He heard one of the metal doors on the pickup clang—was that Pete closing the driver's door, or was it Duane getting in after all?

The pickup screamed into gear, and then the sound of the engine diminished with distance. Kevin lay under the burlap, listening to the truck disappear down the road. Had Duane stayed to keep looking for him? Or had he left with Pete?

He strained for the sound of boots thudding toward the barn again, but he heard nothing. After a silence that seemed to stretch for hours, Kevin heard the rumble of another engine on the road. He listened for the sound of someone hurrying to hide from the other car's view, but nothing moved anywhere near the barn.

How long could he afford to wait? Kevin tried to figure out how much time had passed since Duane had pulled the pin on the grenade. The driving hadn't taken very long, but how long had it taken him to latch the shed and make it to the barn? And how long had he been hiding? It seemed like he'd been buried under the burlap sacking all afternoon, but he knew it hadn't actually been that long. He also knew he couldn't hide forever. If there was a way to stop the fire from happening, he had to try.

Cautiously Kevin slipped his head out from his hiding place. After the thick blackness under the piled sacking, the light spilling through the open side door made the barn seem bright. Kevin glanced around quickly—the barn itself was empty.

He stood up carefully, stretching his cramped muscles, and winced as he straightened his sore knee. It had stiffened up while he had huddled under the burlap.

No Duane sprang through the door at him as Kevin climbed over the tiller and limped hesitantly across the floor. He stood just inside the door listening for a little while, then finally leaned outside and looked around quickly. If Duane was still there, he was hiding too, and Kevin couldn't think of any reason Duane would feel the need to hide from him. He must have left with Pete.

Kevin heaved a sigh of relief. "We're free, Hannibal," he said softly to the hamster, but Hannibal ignored him. "I guess you've had enough excitement for one day," Kevin said. "Stick to your nap."

He headed for the front door of the beat-up house and knocked loudly. He tried several more times, but there was no answer. Duane had been right—everybody must still be at the fair. Kevin made himself try the handle, then try the back door as well. He didn't want to break into someone's house, but if he could get to a phone, he could call Security and get them to stop the grenade.

Kevin checked his watch. He was stunned to discover that he hadn't lost hours inside the barn—only forty-five minutes had passed since they left the frozen grenade at Demolitions. But how long would it take the ice to melt? He couldn't just sit on the front steps and wait for these people to come home.

Kevin looked around helplessly. He caught sight of a rusty bicycle leaning up against the side of the barn. It looked like it was ready for the dump, but the tires were pumped up.

"I'll bring it back," Kevin said aloud, even though there was nobody to hear. "I'm not stealing it—this is an emergency."

He wheeled the bike down to the road. The chain was stiff, the back fender was held on loosely with baling wire, and the wheels squeaked, but at least it was a three-speed. His bad knee had loosened up a little walking around, but he didn't know what kind of time he could make on that thing. Not that he had any other options. Resolutely, Kevin swung his leg over the bar. "Are you ready for this, Hannibal?" he asked, wondering if the hamster was going to get upset at the sudden motion. But he hadn't minded the car ride, after all. The wind might bother him, even through the sweatshirt and flannel pocket. Kevin zipped up his ski jacket and started pedaling.

He stopped at the next farmhouse to hammer on the doors, but there was no one home and no door unlocked, and he had no luck at the next house or the next. Finally

Kevin gave up stopping. It was wasting time, and he couldn't be sure how much he had left. He'd have to put on as much speed as he could and try to reach the Proving Ground gate before the grenade went off.

His knee complained at the constant bending and straightening, but after a little while it got numb and stopped bothering him so much. The bike itself was a different matter. It was a heavy, ancient Schwinn, built to survive the worst sort of treatment and conditions but never intended as a racing bike. It hadn't had much maintenance, either. Kevin didn't think anyone had oiled the chain in years, and each time he tried to shift gears, the cogs screeched and the bike shuddered and he was terrified the chain was about to fall off completely. He decided to coax it up to its fastest gear and just leave it there. It wasn't the most efficient way to make time, but it was probably the safest way to get him to the main gate and the security guard as fast as possible.

He finally turned back onto the main road and started toward the Proving Ground. He shook his watch down to where he could see it below his jacket sleeve—thirty-five more minutes gone. It was only two more miles up to the gate, but now he was biking almost directly into the wind. It rushed, cold and gusting, into his face. The gusts made it impossible to keep up a steady speed, but Kevin was thankful for once for the cold. The colder the wind, the slower the ice would melt.

He pedaled steadily past the fast-rustling cornstalks,

their withered leaves horizontal in the wind. The thought of the flames racing through them made him grit his teeth and pedal harder. He could feel the sweat ice cold on his forehead and trickling hotly down his back. He was burning up inside the heavy jacket. He gulped searing gasps of icy air and wished he could pull the zipper down. But Hannibal was quiet in his pocket, and he didn't dare let the cold wind disturb him. It was all he could do to focus on the white sign marking the Proving Ground gate and concentrate on pumping closer and closer to it. He couldn't handle an unhappy hamster wriggling around trying to get out just then—better to roast. He just wished he could transfer some of that heat to his fingers and face. They felt like blocks of ice.

The thought of ice steadied him, and he forced his legs to keep up the pace. The sign grew larger, slowly but steadily. Two cars passed him, and he wasted precious seconds slowing down and waving at them, trying to get them to stop, but they both swerved around him and punched the gas to hurry away. One of them flipped him the bird as he passed, but Kevin just flipped it back. It's your town, he thought angrily. I ought to let it burn. But he couldn't just shrug it off. If they didn't care, he did.

He wondered if his father had gotten back yet, despite Duane's confidence in the police dispatcher downtown. His father would know what to do about the grenade, he was sure of that. Come on, Dad, be there, Kevin begged silently, pumping the creaking bike as hard as he could.

Finally he reached the gate and swerved inside. He coasted up to the gatehouse, trying to catch his breath, and started in amazement to see Charley Hanson, straddling a pale blue ten-speed, arguing with the Security Guard.

". . . nobody's answering the phone, girlie, okay? And nobody's picking up in the offices either. So what? It's the weekend. What do you want me to do about it?"

"You do something yourself, then," Charley snapped. Her eyes were blazing and, even with her hair tied back in a scarf and tucked inside her coat, Kevin thought she looked more beautiful than ever. "I'm telling you my cousin was here today, maybe he's even still here, and he's up to something bad."

"What do you know about it?" Kevin gasped, his chest still heaving.

Charley spun around to face him. "Where have you been?" she demanded. "We've got to get hold of your father or somebody who can do something around this place!"

The guard sighed. "Okay, kids, beat it now, will you? I've got a job to do."

Kevin glared at him. It was the same guard who'd ignored Duane and Pete on the way out. "If you'd been doing your job earlier, there wouldn't be any problem now!" he said shortly. He reached into his back pocket and hauled out his wallet and showed the guard his ID. "Charley's with me, okay? Look, has my father come in yet?"

The guard shook his head. "No sign of him since he left in your truck about an hour, hour and a half ago. You know, you can't talk to me that way just because you're the Lieutenant Colonel's son, kid."

Kevin felt his heart sink. He hadn't realized how much he'd been counting on his father to take over the problem, to take care of the grenade—to come to his rescue. But wanting his father to be there was as much a waste of time as his willing the guard to stop Duane and Pete in the truck earlier. If anybody was going to do something about the situation, it would have to be him.

He gritted his teeth, shoved the wallet back into his pocket, and tried to keep his voice even. "That wasn't my father, mister. That was two criminals who'd stolen his truck. That means he's probably still downtown at the police station. Call him there, and don't let Jim Dickson put you off. This is an emergency! You've got to get hold of my father and get him up here immediately, if they have to put him in a squad car with the sirens going."

"What the devil are you talking about, kid?" the guard said, his hands on his hips. He made no move to pick up the phone.

"Terrorism," Kevin snapped, his frustration overflowing. "And if you think I'm kidding, if you don't do what I'm telling you to do, you'll be the one responsible when the explosion goes off!"

"What explosion?" the guard demanded, his voice shocked.

Kevin decided he'd wasted enough time and had probably pushed enough of the guard's warning buttons to ensure he'd do his best to get his father.

"Come on, Charley," he said sharply, and headed the bike stiffly into the Proving Ground. He heard her pedals spin and catch, and knew she was following him.

"Hey, hold it right there!" the guard shouted behind them.

"Tell my father to meet us at Point Tango," Kevin called back. "Demolitions. And hurry!"

Kevin pumped as hard as he could on the ancient Schwinn, but Charley coasted up beside him easily.

"You want to tell me what this is all about?" she asked. Her voice was neutral.

"You're the one who said it was about your cousin," Kevin told her, his words coming jerkily between panting breaths. "Why did you say that?"

Charley looked down at her spinning front tire unhappily. "I'm not *sure* it's about Duane," she said slowly.

"So why are you here?" Kevin hated himself for being so cold with her. He wanted to hold her, he wanted to tell her how beautiful she was and to tell her he'd found her great-grandfather's carvings at last—but he couldn't escape the thought that she hated the Proving Ground as much as Duane did. Why had she turned up like that this afternoon? Was she part of Duane's plan? Was she supposed to be some sort of a distraction? Until he knew what part she was playing, he couldn't tell her anything.

Charley downshifted and pedaled steadily beside him

for a few moments. Then she said, "I'm not really sure—I'd have said my family comes first no matter what, but Duane—" She shook her head, her green eyes troubled. "I tried to tell my parents about him, but they never listened. Maybe I didn't try hard enough. Maybe I didn't realize myself just how dangerous he is. But he's scared me now—I think he's got something planned, and if he does, I've got to try to stop him."

"What did he do to scare you?" Kevin asked, a new surge of anger against Duane rising in him. He used it to pump the Schwinn's pedals, hard.

Charley looked at him unhappily. "Duane's been acting even stranger than usual. He kept asking me if I'd be going to the fair today, like he wanted to be sure I'd be downtown. We were at his house last night for supper and I went past his room—the door was partway open, and it looked like a tornado had hit the place."

She shook her head, frowning, and her breath came unevenly as she pedaled to keep up with him. "All his camouflage gear was lying all over the place—his entire collection of *Soldier of Fortune* magazines was all over the floor, open to different articles—then he caught me looking, and he was really furious. He yelled at me, wanted to know why I was messing with his things." She paused for breath. "I've been in and out of Duane's house hundreds of times, and he's never gotten mad at me like that before."

"So?" Kevin swung down the road he remembered from earlier. He wondered how close they actually were to Point Tango. If they didn't get there in time to stop the explosion, how far would the phosphorus shoot? He winced and tried to pedal harder.

"So Duane's gotten crazier than ever," Charley snapped breathlessly. "Since that Pete Elliott moved to town, it's like Duane's gotten angrier. He's never been too tightly wired to reality. He used to read those magazines all the time and dream a lot, and he'd say things, but he was all talk."

"What about the military cars he messed up?" Kevin demanded.

Charley shook her head sharply and pedaled in silence for a few moments. When she answered, her voice had a trace of its old edge. "Okay, he's always been a bully. Is that what you wanted to hear? Yeah, he's always threatened other kids with his knife, and he got his kicks out of putting dents into cars with military stickers, but mostly he was talk. His buddies used to kid him about it—Duane could dream up any plan, they'd say. But he didn't carry them out."

"And since Pete got here?"

"I think Pete was egging him on," Charley said slowly, "like a little kid daring another kid to do something. He was the one who talked Duane into making those terrorist threats, you know. Duane always talked about getting revenge on the Proving Ground, but I think Pete frightened him."

"Frightened of Pete?" Kevin couldn't help the incredulity in his voice.

"No," Charley said impatiently, punctuating her words with hard pumps on her bike pedals, "frightened of growing up and never doing anything but talk. His parents wanted him to go to college, but he wouldn't apply. He said he didn't want to leave Hadley and all his buddies. The only thing he really wanted to do was get even with the Proving Ground and be a big hero in Hadley."

"What about you?" Kevin asked, coasting suddenly. "Will you ever be able to leave Hadley behind, or do you have to get even with the Proving Ground somehow too?"

"Me?" Charley sounded shocked. "I'm not like Duane!"

"You're not crazy," Kevin agreed, then pedaled on in silence.

"We've both got plenty of reasons to hate the Proving Ground," Charley said sharply.

Kevin shrugged. All he said was, "You both have the same great-grandfather." He knew it was important that they talk about this, but now that he knew Charley wasn't part of Duane's plan, he was only giving the conversation half of his attention. The rest of his mind was focused on the frozen grenade. He kept seeing ice cubes poured into the kitchen sink. They melted awfully fast. The image was enough to make him force his aching legs to speed up.

Charley frowned at her bike handles. "My great-grandfather stood up for what he believed," she said between short breaths. "I've always wanted to do the same thing. But Duane's not like him at all. This plan to get even—that's not going to change anything about Great-grandfather."

She shifted gears and caught up with him, and her voice turned hard. "And it wasn't even really Duane's plan! Pete came along and told Duane he'd never get even, all he'd ever do was talk about it. I think Duane got scared of being out of school and having all the guys he used to brag to pointing at him and saying, 'Look at him—he was going to close down the Proving Ground and be a big hero,' and laughing at him."

"So he had to do something," Kevin said. He realized they'd been talking together almost as though they were friends. He glanced over to take a quick look at her face and she smiled a little at him. He felt the heat rising in his neck as he smiled back.

"Pete had some of the seniors laughing at him already," Charley went on, her smile fading. "I think Duane convinced himself his only choice was to actually do what he'd bragged about—I think he's planned out some mission, and I think he picked today, when most of the town would be busy at the fair and it would be easier to get in and out of the Proving Ground."

Kevin stopped as the uneven road intersected the road that ran parallel to the testing areas and looked around, breathing in uneven gasps.

"Where are we?" Charley asked, trying to catch her own breath.

"I hope we're near Point Tango," Kevin said, studying

the land. "I've only been there once." He stole a quick glance at her. "Duane brought me."

"Duane!" Her eyes widened. "I was right!"

Kevin nodded. "You were right about his mission. I just hope we're in time to stop it. Come on, I think we go this way."

The bikes bounced and jolted over the uneven concrete, but they reached Point Tango in a couple of minutes. Kevin jumped off the still coasting bike and let it fall behind him.

"What's all this straw for?" Charley asked. "And what am I smelling? Diesel?"

"I think your cousin would call it eau de arson," Kevin said, remembering. He caught sight of the grenade and felt his mouth dry up. "Charley—get back!"

He felt her following him. "What is it?"

"Get back!" he shouted, reaching behind him and shoving her. "Way back, in case it blows!"

"What?" she screamed, but he heard her backing away.

The grenade still stood where Duane had placed it. The last of the melting ice somehow held the bail down, and Kevin couldn't believe it hadn't gone off yet. He crept closer, terrified of shaking the ground or stepping on the wrong piece of straw and pulling it the slightest bit and causing the grenade to tip over. That would be enough to shake off the remaining ice and release the bail, he was sure of it. If he could just get hold of it and squeeze the bail down—

"Kevin, what is that thing?" Charley's voice was

steady, but he could hear she'd done what he said. He still didn't know how far back would be safe, but he thought she sounded far enough away.

"It's Duane's mission," he called to her, and reached for the grenade.

≡ **12** ≡

OUT ON A LIMB

The shrunken chunk of ice surrounding the grenade shimmered wetly in the chill light, and Kevin had a sudden vision of the ice slipping away and setting off the explosion just before his hand reached the metal. Then he touched the slick surface. For an instant, he thought his vision was about to come true as the ice cracked under his fingers and fell away from the grenade. But his hand was already clenched tightly around the slippery metal.

His chest hurt, and Kevin realized he had stopped breathing some time before. He drew in a shuddering breath thick with the smell of the diesel and squeezed the bail against the body of the grenade as hard as possible. He felt Hannibal yawn hugely in his pocket and then settle back comfortably, and he almost laughed. Not taking his eyes off the grenade, he slowly got to his feet and turned around.

"Charley?" he called. His throat felt dry, but his voice didn't crack, and he felt a flicker of pleasure.

"Is it okay now?" she asked. He could hear her footsteps hurrying closer.

"It will be soon," he told her, not letting his attention

slip away from the grenade. Somewhere in the distance he thought he could hear a siren, but sound was funny. It might be his father, if the Security Guard had put enough pressure on the police. But the siren could still be a long way off. He couldn't depend on the police.

Could he hold on to the icy grenade until someone got there? Despite the cold, his right hand was slick with perspiration, and the metal of the grenade was slippery in his grasp. Suppose he lost his grip and it slipped out of his hand? The bail would fly up and Duane would have succeeded in his mission after all, even down to making sure there were no witnesses. If the grenade went off, he and Charley would never get the chance to tell anyone who the terrorists really were. Kevin shuddered inwardly at the thought.

How could he secure the bail? Kevin remembered Duane crouching there on the ground, twirling the pin on its ring around his finger. Had he tossed it down? Kevin couldn't remember.

"Charley," he said, "can you see a pin for this on the ground anywhere? It would have a ring on one end, about the size of a quarter, and then two prongs poking out from it."

"Shiny?" she asked, scanning the ground.

"No, dull green like this," he said, gesturing very slightly with the grenade.

She looked hard, sifting through the straw with her fingers, but nothing turned up.

"No luck," she announced finally.

Duane must have taken it with him, Kevin thought. His mind raced—what could he do now?

"Would something else do?" she asked. "Something stiff, like the straw?"

Kevin looked up, frowning worriedly. "No, the straw would break, but something like that."

Charley looked around, her hands on her hips. She scanned the ground, then studied her bike. Suddenly her face lit up. "What about that bike of yours?" she demanded. "The back fender's held on with baling wire. Would a piece of that do?"

"Yeah," Kevin said, relieved. "It should be thin enough."

Charley hurried to the rusty bike lying on the ground. Kevin thought about the unexpected change in her attitude toward him. Suddenly they were a team, no sparks flying, no shouting, just trying to work together. He wondered if it could always be like this from now on. Maybe so—he hadn't even told her about the carvings yet, he reminded himself.

"How big a piece do you need, Kevin?" she called.

Kevin smiled a little. No more "Army brat" either, it seemed. "Any length," he told her, "so long as you can twist it off easily. I just need to put it through the hole where the pin was. Then this thing can't go off."

He had a sudden worry about the wire on the bike. What if Charley couldn't twist a piece of it off? Or, if she could, what would he do if the wire turned out to be too thick to fit through the pinholes after all?

The siren sounded closer now. Kevin wondered vaguely whether they'd turned in to the Proving Ground yet. It wouldn't be much longer now, one way or the other. Between the frozen metal of the grenade and the cold wind gusts, his right hand was growing so cold the fingers felt numb. He wrapped his left hand around the white knuckles to make sure his fingers didn't weaken and slip. He seemed to feel the bail pressing hard against his hand, straining to break free. It was just his imagination, of course. There wasn't that much force in the lever's spring. But he couldn't shake the feeling.

"Here." Charley was standing right in front of him, holding out a crooked piece of wire about six inches long. "Will this do it?"

Kevin nodded. "Perfect." He took his left hand off the cold right one and reached out to take the wire. Then he smiled at her slightly. "Just in case I screw it all up now, you'd better get back where it's safe."

"You won't," she said encouragingly, but she backed off to where she'd stood before.

Kevin looked at the grenade. The pinhole suddenly seemed impossibly small. He took the thin wire and poked it through, but it wouldn't go. Stop shaking, he ordered his hands angrily. He tried again, but the wire refused to go all the way through.

Confused, Kevin turned the grenade slightly, careful not to weaken his grip on the bail. Was the wire too thick after all? He tried to sight through the holes, but the light didn't come through as a neat circle. It was more like a narrow slit. Something had to be blocking the opening. Then he realized he hadn't lined the holes up together—the bail was pressed so tightly against the body of the grenade that its pinhole was half blocked. He would have to loosen his hand and let the lever up slightly.

Kevin swallowed. If the grenade was going to go off, this would be the time. He carefully relaxed his stiff fingers, very slightly, hoping to ease the bail up. He was afraid his numb fingers would come apart entirely and the bail would fly up. But their tension held. He watched the slit of light widen slowly as the pinholes crept into alignment, until he could see a neat circle. Quickly he slipped the wire into the first hole, wiggled it slightly, and popped it through the far end.

He couldn't believe it was done. In the end the wire had slipped through almost ridiculously easily. He awkwardly used his left hand to bend the loose ends together around the outside of the pinhole, twisting the wire again and again to make sure there was no way it could work itself loose accidentally. Then he eased his grip on the bail. He kept expecting the bail to trick him, to spring back at him without warning. But the wire held, and finally his hand was open, the grenade lying loosely in his icy palm.

Kevin looked up from the grenade to meet Charley's eyes. Wordlessly, they smiled at each other.

Kevin realized the siren had grown much louder. He heard tires throwing up gravel, and suddenly a police car slewed to a stop near them and the doors burst open.

"Kevin?" LTC Spencer shouted, and broke into a run. Then he saw the grenade lying in Kevin's hand. His voice sharpened abruptly to the one he saved for issuing orders. "Don't move, Kevin, I'll be right there—don't move."

Kevin turned toward him, grinning. "It's okay, Dad," he called. "It's safe now—I stopped it."

"What in the world—" his father started, then shook his head as Kevin handed him the secured grenade. He looked back and forth from Kevin to the grenade to the ground strewn with the diesel-soaked straw for a few moments, then fixed his eye on his son.

"I think you'd better tell me exactly what's been going on here," LTC Spencer said. Even standing there in his blue jeans and sheepskin jacket, he was no longer a father talking to his son. He had turned into an officer investigating a crisis situation. "Miller called the police and demanded I be rushed up here because the Proving Ground was under terrorist attack—and said you ordered him to!"

Kevin nodded, trying to report dispassionately. "That's right. Those guys who stole the pickup? They're the ones who were making terrorist threats. They used our truck with its ID sticker to get past Security and they set that white-phosphorus grenade in ice to go off when the ice melted so it would start a fire. See all the straw? They poured diesel on it to make sure the fire took off. Then they drove the pickup out the front gate the same way they came in. Miller said he thought it was you."

LTC Spencer was frowning, plainly incredulous. "Are you telling me the truth, Kevin? How could you possibly know all this?"

"Of course he's telling the truth," Charley blurted out. She flushed and frowned at her feet. "Kevin wouldn't lie to you."

LTC Spencer studied Charley briefly. Then he asked Kevin, "Who is this?"

"This is Charley Hanson, Dad," he said, and added, "She's a friend of mine from school."

"And what do you know about this, Miss Hanson?" LTC Spencer asked.

"I know he's telling the truth," she told him. "And I know who set the grenade, just as well as Kevin does."

"Who are these terrorists?" LTC Spencer's voice was expressionless.

Kevin hesitated, stole a quick look at Charley, and opened his mouth.

"Duane Hanson and Pete Elliott," Charley's voice echoed his as he spoke.

"What?" LTC Spencer's eyes flicked from Kevin to Charley. She lifted her chin and stared evenly at him.

"Duane is my cousin," she told him flatly, "and he's been planning to get even with the Proving Ground for a long time. I finally put it together that today was the day he'd picked to do it, because the Art Fair would keep everybody downtown—but I never dreamed he'd do anything so—so—*extreme*."

Between the two of them, the story of Duane's mission poured out. Taking turns, they each told him about Duane's planning, Pete's egging him on, Duane's threats in the school parking lot, and the part Kevin had played.

When it was all over, LTC Spencer stood still a few moments. Then he summarized, "Kevin, are you willing to testify that Duane and Pete threatened one month ago to get the Army out of Hadley in a month's time, stated that they made terrorist threats to the Proving Ground, stole our truck, broke into our quarters and destroyed the place, abducted you without provocation, arranged this explosion with the intention of burning a section of the Proving Ground to include the Housing Area, and attempted first to frame you and then to kill you?"

Kevin felt a flush rising. He'd known he'd have to explain sooner or later. "Yes, Sir, all but the abduction part, exactly."

His father frowned. "Go on."

"They didn't know I was in the house at first," he explained. "I meant to stay hidden in the attic, but"—he avoided his father's sudden start of surprise and blurted out, "they smashed up Hannibal's cage and hurt him and I came down to stop them."

"You what?" The color ran out of LTC Spencer's face.

"I came down to stop them," Kevin repeated stubbornly. Why couldn't his father stop being an officer for a few minutes, and quit running things and telling people what to do, and just be a father? "I couldn't just sit there and let them hurt a little animal. I surprised Duane and Pete, and then I found Hannibal. He was terrified."

"You should have had the sense to be terrified too," his father snapped. "Didn't it occur to you that you were unarmed and those thugs were dangerous?"

Kevin nodded. "Yes, Sir."

"Why didn't you stay put?" his father demanded.

"And let Hannibal be killed?" Kevin returned hotly. "I had to do something! There was nobody else who could help Hannibal. I know it was risky, but I had to do it!"

"You could have been killed," LTC Spencer said flatly. Kevin looked at his father's face. Underneath the anger he could see the worry—and also the fear. He's mad because I could have been hurt, he realized, because he could have lost me. It's not that he wants me to be a wimp all my life.

"I had to do it," Kevin repeated.

LTC Spencer closed his eyes for a moment. When he opened them, he looked directly at Kevin. "Is Hannibal all right?"

Kevin managed a ghostly smile. "He's fine."

His father nodded, once. "I understand. What you did today—it took a lot of courage." Kevin could see an odd brightness in his father's eyes as they studied him. "I'm proud of you, Kevin."

Kevin forgot Charley standing there with them. All he could see was his father's approval, and his love.

Then Kevin said awkwardly, "I only did what you've always done, Dad."

"What?" LTC Spencer asked, surprised.

"You've always stood up for what you believed in," Kevin explained.

A sudden shadow fell over his father's face. "Not always," he said bitterly. "Not since we came to Hadley."

"But you have," Kevin disagreed. At his father's surprised expression he explained, "I know the testing's bogus and the Colonel won't stop it, and I know you've been going out on a limb trying to change things—Chris Waverly told me that. He even threatened me to make you stop. I never told you because I knew threats wouldn't make any difference to you. You'd do what's right."

LTC Spencer sighed. "What's right isn't always as easy to see as rescuing Hannibal. It's time for me to make decisions—" He seemed to remember Charley suddenly, and changed the subject. "But that isn't your problem." He included Charley in his look. "The problem for the two of you is going to be testifying against those two boys. Kevin, I believe you can handle it, but what about you, Miss Hanson, or may I call you Charley? This boy is your cousin—can you testify against him?"

Charley looked outraged. "What he did was wrong!"

"What if the rest of your family doesn't see it that way?" LTC Spencer asked gently. "What will you do if they're disappointed in you and feel you've betrayed them?"

Charley stared at him, a wretched expression on her face. Kevin's heart went out to her. But he still knew she'd stand up for what she believed in. She always had.

"They might, you know," LTC Spencer told her, his voice sad. "Some of them might, at least."

"I know some of them will," she said, her stubbornness dissolving into unhappiness. Kevin thought she was thinking about Duane's parents, who never believed anything bad about their son. "But I'd have to do it anyway."

Kevin's father nodded slowly. The three of them were quiet for a few minutes. Then Charley turned away and started for her bike. "Look, I'd better get home."

"Wait," Kevin said quickly. "Charley—I wanted to tell you—I found something of yours in the attic today."

Charley stopped, one foot balanced on her bike pedal. "Mine? In the attic? You can't have found anything of mine."

Kevin thought he heard a ghost of her old hostility, but he decided to ignore it. "I meant what I told you before, in school—I've been looking for the carving your great-grandfather was working on. And I found it."

"Dad said the attic used to be Great-grandfather's workshop," Charley said slowly. "But there can't be anything left in it. We got his tools and stuff when they unloaded the house."

"He hid this," Kevin said. "He probably didn't want your dad finding it and spoiling the surprise. But I found it, and now it's yours."

"What is it?"

Kevin could see in her eyes just how much she wanted to know, but he shook his head. "I can't tell you," he said. "You've got to see it for yourself."

He looked at his father, then back at Charley. "Look, the house is a real wreck with the things they broke and the fuel oil everywhere. I don't think we should be going inside for anything—"

"Definitely not," his father agreed, "until we check it and make sure there's no danger, especially from the fuel oil." Then he grinned at Kevin. "Besides, if you're so worried about Hannibal, I don't think the fumes would be any good for him."

"He didn't like the smell much at all," Kevin agreed. "So I was thinking, Charley—Dad and I could get the carving out tonight, and I'll meet you tomorrow and give it to you then. The house will probably still smell awful, and you probably wouldn't want to go there anyway, but how about the school parking lot?"

"Okay." Charley nodded. "I'll meet you there after lunch, at one."

She started to pedal away, then coasted to a stop. "I can't stand it—who, or what, is Hannibal?"

Kevin and his father looked at each other and laughed, like the old days. Kevin unzipped his jacket and, standing with his back to the wind, tugged his sweatshirt up. He unbuttoned his pocket and peered down.

"Hey, in there, you want to come out and say hi? You've been sleeping forever."

There was a rustle of movement, and Hannibal poked his head up from under the pocket flap, his bright black eyes squinting in the light. Then he felt the cold air and ducked back inside the pocket.

"He likes it warm and dark," Kevin explained. He waited, knowing how blunt Charley was. He half-expected her to tell him how weird it was to have a hamster at his age.

Instead, Charley shook her head slowly. "A hamster?" she demanded, smiling. "You are full of surprises, Kevin Spencer."

As she pedaled away, Kevin heard her muttering, "A hamster. . . ."

☰ 13 ☰

GREAT-GRANDFATHER'S CARVINGS

Charley was waiting for him in the school parking lot. She was sitting on the low concrete wall beside the stairs, looking out toward the football field with her hair flying loose in the breeze and her heels impatiently drumming on the wall. Kevin thought she looked like someone who had far better things to do on a Sunday afternoon than hang around a parking lot waiting for him to show up.

He got off his bike and walked it slowly across the asphalt toward her, favoring his sore knee only slightly. It hurt far less than it had the day before, when Pete bashed it. The ticking of the wheels seemed impossibly loud in his ears, but she didn't notice him until he had almost reached her. As soon as she saw him, she jumped down from the wall and dusted her hands off on her jeans.

"Hi," he said. He wondered whether they'd still feel any of the easy camaraderie they'd had yesterday, or if he'd be demoted to the Army brat again.

"Hi," she said.

They stood for a few moments, not sure what to say.

"How's Hannibal?" Charley finally asked.

Kevin grinned. "He's okay. We couldn't stay in the quarters last night, we had to stay in a motel, but I got his exercise wheel and his food dish and some stuff and put him in the bathtub at the motel on a towel. He sat in his food dish and quivered for a while, but then he started running in his wheel and messing around like normal. He didn't try to escape from the tub, though—I think he's had enough of away-from-home adventures for a while."

She laughed. "He's a spunky little guy."

"He is that," Kevin agreed.

"I'm glad your father finally understood why you rescued him," Charley said. "But he shouldn't have been so surprised."

"What do you mean?" Kevin looked at her, surprised himself.

Charley shrugged. "I could have told him you'd jump down to save Hannibal. You care about things," she explained. "You cared about Hannibal, and you cared about Hadley, enough to stop the grenade yourself. And I could even see how much you cared about your father. He should have figured it out."

"Yeah, well . . ." Kevin got busy setting his kickstand and leaving his bike next to hers, ducking his head so his blush wouldn't be quite so obvious. He wondered if she knew who else he cared about. After a few seconds he asked, "How'd it go last night?"

She sighed. "Federal agents came and asked me a lot of questions. They said they'd arrested Duane after he got home. My aunt was on the phone in hysterics to my mother. She kept saying he hadn't done anything and he was with friends and could prove it, and she tried to tell the police that, but they took him away anyhow. And she screamed a lot about what a liar and a traitor I was." She shot him a quick glance and then looked away.

"They picked up Pete, and he spilled everything, saying it was all Duane's idea, of course. So now Duane's locked up without bail and they're going to be moving him out of Hadley to a federal prison. Apparently on top of what he did to you, what he tried to do to the Proving Ground is a big deal."

Kevin nodded. "Trying to blow up a military base is like trying to blow up Congress or the White House. It's a federal crime."

Charley looked angry. "What gets me is that it was so stupid!" she cried. "Even if his plan had worked, it wouldn't have helped my great-grandfather any! Nobody in Washington would have apologized or tried to make amends or anything."

"I don't think it had anything to do with your great-grandfather in the end," Kevin said slowly. "I think in the end it was all about Duane himself, like you said—about his being scared of never doing anything. I think he wanted to be a hero." Kevin thought he could even understand that feeling—it wasn't all that different from the way he had felt himself.

"Well, it was a stupid way to try to be a hero," Charley snapped.

"True," Kevin agreed. He unslung his backpack with the carvings inside. "And I don't think your great-grandfather would have approved of it either."

"What do you know about my great-grandfather?" Charley demanded, flaring up the way she always had. But Kevin was beginning to think maybe she was always this way, with people she liked as well as military people she thought she hated.

"I know a little more about him than I did yesterday morning," Kevin said, pulling the wooden case from the attic out of his backpack. "Before I found this," he added.

He held it out to her. "Go on, Charley, take it—it's yours now."

Charley reached for the box and cradled it gently in her arms. Kevin watched her run her fingers over the satiny wood. He wondered suddenly if he should leave her alone to open it in private, but he couldn't go. He wanted to see her reaction. And there were a few more things he wanted to tell her. She laid the old box respectfully down on the concrete ledge, then felt with her fingers for the catch. She neatly slipped the small hook and raised the fitted lid, and then she just stood there, her eyes widening, staring at the rows of neat little figures each lying in its own little niche.

It was a collection of toy soldiers, a set of perfectly carved miniature models of American soldiers from the battles and wars throughout the country's history. The first was a Minuteman, and Zouaves, from the Revolutionary War, and defenders of Washington from the War of 1812, cavalry officers from the Indian Wars, both Union and Confederate soldiers from the Civil War— soldiers going all the way up through World War I, the last war that old Duane Hanson knew of. The final row was a series of larger niches with mounted soldiers.

"Toy soldiers?" Charley said softly, her voice incredulous.

"Toy soldiers," Kevin agreed. "Maybe your dad liked playing with soldiers, and your great-grandfather thought he'd teach him a little history while he was at it. I showed them to my father and he said they looked pretty accurate to him."

Charley looked up at him, her green eyes clouded with confusion. "But—soldiers—Great-grandfather didn't like—"

Kevin shook his head. "I know he's your great-grandfather, not mine, but I think we both made a mistake in trying to understand him." Charley's eyes lost their confusion and flashed angrily, but Kevin went on.

"Hold it a minute, will you?" He tried to choose his words carefully. "Your great-grandfather gave an interview about the land-appropriation thing. He said he was angry at the government bureaucracy that ran over everybody without bothering to pay attention to details or to find out the real story." Kevin thought that the bureaucracy wasn't the only one that hadn't bothered to find out the real story—the Hansons had done their share of closing their eyes to the truth over the years—but he kept the thought to himself.

"It wasn't the Army at all," he went on. "He even said that he respected the Army and he understood that the Army needed places to test their ammunition. He just resented the way Hadley had been treated and wanted a forum to speak out about it."

Charley was quiet for a few minutes, her fingers lightly exploring the soldiers. She picked up the small World War I infantryman and turned him over in her hands, studying the details of the carving. Kevin looked with her. "The infantryman," he said, "he's beautiful. He reminds me of the fighter you had at the Dungeons & Dragons meeting."

Charley jerked her head sharply. "No way—this is much better. See the detail on the face? And the way his hands hold his rifle? I can't begin to do beautiful detail work like that." She sighed, still turning the soldier over and over in her hands. "You tried to tell me, after school that day, before Duane showed up. You said it was all about the bureaucracy, not the Army."

Kevin nodded, remembering shouting at her, trying to get through to her.

"So—is your father going to find a forum to speak out about the Proving Ground?" she asked, laying the infantryman down and picking up a Union cavalry officer from the Civil War.

"He and Mom were still up discussing it last night when I fell asleep," Kevin said. He grinned a little. "Between their talking and Hannibal's wheel squeaking, it was a pretty noisy motel room." His smile faded. "But this morning Dad told me he's decided to take the problem to TECOM headquarters—that's the command division that's responsible for the Proving Ground. He wants to try to get them to realize what's going on here with the falsified test reports and have them assign a new commanding officer who can take charge and fix it."

"Does that mean he thinks he can get things changed?" Charley asked.

Kevin shrugged. "It means he's made up his mind that the only way to ever get any changes made is for someone to speak out about the problem. He said there's a risk that they might not listen and he's the one who could get reassigned." He smiled slightly. "It's his way of marching to the sound of the guns in peacetime," he said softly.

Charley didn't ask what he meant. She just laid the cavalry officer back in his niche. "All those years," she said, shaking her head, "this was waiting for somebody to find it. It's like Great-grandfather was waiting for us to figure it all out, and get on with our lives."

Kevin nodded. "That's what I meant when I said I didn't think your great-grandfather would have approved of Duane's plan. Revenge against the Army and the Proving Ground wasn't what he was interested in. He was angry with the bureaucracy and wanted to try to put pressure on it to perform more fairly, and that's a whole different problem."

Kevin zipped up his empty backpack and slung it over his shoulder. "So—you've got the missing carvings now—I've got to go. Maybe we can stop arguing all the time, though?" He started for his bike. He didn't want to ask yet if they could be friends.

"Wait, Kevin," she said quickly. "I—I brought something for you." She flipped her hair back, unzipped her shoulder bag, dug inside, and came up with a small plain box. She handed it to him.

Kevin took it carefully, feeling a surge of hope. Maybe it would be more than just not fighting all the time— maybe that was what she wanted to tell him. He opened the box.

Lying inside was a carved figure of a fierce ranger wearing studded leather armor, with a short sword hanging from his belt. A quiver of arrows hung over his left shoulder, and he carried a bow.

"Orion," Kevin whispered.

"I remembered your saying your character was a ranger that first afternoon when you came to the Dungeons & Dragons meeting," she said quickly. "I didn't know if you played with models in your old group—not every group does. I had the figure roughed out already, but I didn't know yet what he was going to be. After yesterday afternoon, I worked on him all last night and this morning to finish him for you. I figured you'd need him if you were going to play with us here."

Kevin looked up at her quickly. "I didn't think I was welcome."

Charley made an impatient gesture. "Look—I'm trying to say I'm sorry," she told him fiercely. "I made a mistake, okay? I don't make mistakes very often, but I made one when you came here. I made a mistake about you and, I guess"—her voice lost its sharpness and became almost bewildered as she looked back at her great-grandfather's carvings—"I made one about my great-grandfather. So I'm trying to apologize." She looked up at him. "Will you come back to Dungeons & Dragons?"

Kevin frowned a little. "I really love the carving and I accept your apology, but there are other Hadley kids who don't want me around either—it might be better if—"

"Well, they've made a mistake too," Charley interrupted. "And if anybody objects, I'll tell them so."

Kevin grinned at the image of her fighting *for* him instead of sizing up her best opportunity for beating the stuffing out of him.

"I guess I owe you an apology too," he told her. "I'm sorry about calling you Chuck—I was just kind of steamed."

She grinned. "Fair enough."

They looked at each other for a minute, then each of them dropped their eyes, feeling awkward.

"So." Charley cleared her throat. "You'll keep the ranger and come to Dungeons & Dragons?"

Kevin closed the box, pulled off his backpack, and zipped the small ranger safely inside. "You realize we might not be here long?" he asked. "If Dad runs into trouble at TECOM, he could be reassigned right away."

Charley made a face. "Well, I hope that doesn't happen, but for however long you stay in Hadley, Kevin, I really want you to come to Dungeons & Dragons."

Kevin smiled. After all, joining the Math Club had turned out to be a success. And he wasn't the same Kevin Spencer who had moved to Hadley, the guy who didn't know how to stand up for himself. Andy would be in Dungeons & Dragons also, he reminded himself, razzing him about liking Charley and backing him up if any of the other kids got nasty.

And he'd finally gotten what he wanted from the first—Charley, giving him her full attention.

"Okay, Charley," he said. "You win—I'll come."

Her smile lit her entire face and warmed her brilliant green eyes, and Kevin knew it didn't matter what happened with TECOM. Whatever time his family had left in Hadley, he and Charley would have together.

AUTHOR'S NOTE

This is a work of fiction. Hadley Proving Ground does not exist. There are seven Proving Grounds scattered across the United States in which the Army tests its ammunition and equipment before issuing them to troops in the field. Many military installations have had land-appropriation problems in their past that have resulted in condemnation suits like the one involving the Hansons. However, Mr. Hanson's death in court as it occurs in this novel is entirely a fictional incident.

On a cautionary note, military armaments are tightly regulated and should be handled only by highly trained personnel within a controlled context. It is both dangerous and illegal to possess any live hand grenade, and civilian handling of a grenade is strongly discouraged.

I would like to thank my friend and colleague, Sandy Asher, for her assistance and encouragement on this project.

I would also like to thank my editor, Simone Kaplan, for her hard work and insightful comments which helped turn my manuscript into this book.

Finally, I would like to thank Lieutenant Colonel (Ret.) Arthur B. Alphin. As an Army officer, he shared with me his invaluable expertise in weapons technology and his wealth of personal military experience. As my husband, he patiently and critically read many versions of this manuscript and unwaveringly supported me throughout the book's completion.